CLEVER CREATURES OF THE NIGHT

CLEVER CREATURES OF THE NIGHT

A NOVEL BY

SAMANTHA MABRY

ALGONQUIN YOUNG READERS

WORKMAN PUBLISHING

NEW YORK

Copyright © 2024 by Samantha Mabry

Hachette Book Group supports the right to free expression and the value of copyright. The purpose of copyright is to encourage writers and artists to produce the creative works that enrich our culture.

The scanning, uploading, and distribution of this book without permission is a theft of the author's intellectual property. If you would like permission to use material from the book (other than for review purposes), please contact permissions@hbgusa.com. Thank you for your support of the author's rights.

Algonquin Young Readers
Workman Publishing
Hachette Book Group, Inc.
1290 Avenue of the Americas
New York, NY 10104
workman.com

Algonquin Young Readers is an imprint of Workman Publishing, a division of Hachette Book Group, Inc. The Workman name and logo are registered trademarks of Hachette Book Group, Inc.

Design by Kayla E.

The publisher is not responsible for websites (or their content) that are not owned by the publisher.

The Hachette Speakers Bureau provides a wide range of authors for speaking events. To find out more, go to hachettespeakersbureau.com or email HachetteSpeakers@hbgusa.com.

Workman books may be purchased in bulk for business, educational, or promotional use. For information, please contact your local bookseller or the Hachette Book Group Special Markets Department at special.markets@hbgusa.com.

LIBRARY OF CONGRESS CATALOGING-IN-PUBLICATION DATA

Names: Mabry, Samantha, author.
Title: Clever creatures of the night / a novel by Samantha Mabry.
Description: First edition. | New York : Algonquin Young Readers, 2024. |
Audience: Ages 14 and up. | Audience: Grades 10-12. | Summary: When Case arrives at her best friend Drea's isolated West Texas home and finds her missing, she embarks on a search for clues about Drea's disappearance while facing the unsettling, cult-like and possibly murderous behavior of Drea's roommates.
Identifiers: LCCN 2023032945 | ISBN 9781616208974 (hardcover) |
ISBN 9781523527465 (ebook)
Subjects: CYAC: Missing persons—Fiction. | Friendship—Fiction. |
Roommates—Fiction. | Texas—Fiction. | LCGFT: Novels.
Classification: LCC PZ7.1.M244 Cl 2024 | DDC [Fic]—dc23
LC record available at https://lccn.loc.gov/2023032945

First Edition March 2024 LSC-C

Printed in the USA on responsibly sourced paper.

10 9 8 7 6 5 4 3 2 1

hachette
BOOK GROUP

Customer Service: 1-800-759-0190
customer.service@hbgusa.com

BILL TO:
COMPLIMENTARY ORDERS
HACHETTE BOOK GROUP
53 STATE ST

BOSTON. MA 02109

PACKING LIST
02/08/2024

SHIP TO:
MARCIA MARQUES
495 W SOUTH ORANGE AVE

SOUTH ORANGE, NJ 07079

CUST #: 19700086

0623

ORD'D	SHIP'D	ITEM	TITLE		PRICE	DISC
			PO# 2224cc	Invoice# 74502566	Order Ref# 2402202112/001	
1	1	9781616208974	CLEVER CREATURES OF THE NIGHT		$.00	0

Item courtesy of Workman Publishing
OT86 apprd by Lyndsay 6811728 moek 2/2 341p

EXT. TOTAL: $.00

Shortages and Damage Claims must be made 30 days from Invoice Date. Prices subject
to change without notice. Whole Copy Returns should be sent to Hachette Book Group
322 South Enterprise Blvd Lebanon, IN 46052. Stripped Cover Returns should be sent

AGAIN, FOR MY STUDENTS

CLEVER CREATURES OF THE NIGHT

PART ONE:

DAY

EIGHT

ALL THE EARLY MORNINGS LOOK LIKE THIS: The distant hills are shrouded by a dull gray murk. The trees are frozen in their stark stances. The sky is so thick and ash-colored that it's impossible to tell what kinds of birds soar silently by until they let out their small, distinguishable cries. When the sun finally hauls itself up and over the zigzag horizon, its weak light is tissue-paper pink.

Is this beautiful or not?

Case rolls down the window to get a better view of those shrouded, distant hills and is immediately hit with the smell of a trash fire. She jolts back in her seat. The scent of smoldering wood alongside the sharp reek of melting plastic is so fresh and familiar. Someone is always burning something out here, even though the county has banned fires.

Case catches the concerned look of the driver in the rearview mirror. "It's the air," she says.

"Hmm." The man crinkles his nose. "I've never been down this road."

The driver is maybe only five years older than Case, but he has a row of pictures of his family taped up on his dashboard. There's a toddler girl seated on a red tricycle, and an older boy in ready position next to a T-ball stand. Several times during this drive, forty miles westward from Fort Worth, Case has noticed him reaching out to tap the faces on those photos with the fingers of his right hand. He does it again, right now. Is it some kind of good luck tic? Are his kids somewhere far away and he has convinced himself that touching their frozen faces will bring them closer? Or maybe any amount of time away from them feels too long, and his fingers always itch to touch their skin.

"Before I came to pick you up, I double-checked the address to make sure," the driver says. "Even if you look at the satellite, there's nothing but trees."

"I did the same thing," Case replies, rolling up her window. "Looked at the satellite, I mean."

When someone grows up in a rural county, they know all the roads, even the ones they've never gone down. And since this is the county in which Case grew up, she knew this road was here, but she had always assumed it led to some long-collapsed farmhouse or dead-ended into a riverbank. At the turnoff, there wasn't a sign or street numbers, or even a mailbox. There was fencing, but it had clearly been neglected for a long time. The wire was snapped and bright with rust. The wood posts were split and slanted.

But the directions in Andrea's letter were as clear as they could be, and typical for a house tucked deep into the woods: *Turn right at the first road after you cross the north fork of the river. Go down farther than you think. The trees will get thicker. The road will get narrower. Keep going. There's a curve. The house is green.*

As the trees get thicker and the road gets narrower, the driver shifts forward in his seat, his chest hovering an inch from the steering wheel. The road starts to feel like it's dissolving into the oaks and dying cedars, but then, finally, it curves—just as Andrea had said it would—and the house comes into view.

"Oh," the driver says, straightening up suddenly. "This is it? Are you sure this is it? Someone lives here?"

Case doesn't reply. She was expecting the house to be green because of paint, but that's not right. It's green because it's covered in ivy. The sides of the old house might be bricked or covered in long strips of siding, but from a distance, it's impossible to tell. Most of the windows— both on the first and second story—are almost completely obscured by leaves and vines. Wooden steps that lead up to the front door are cracked in half, as if someone had gone and smashed them with a bat. At some point, bricks came loose from the chimney—dislodged probably by that creeping ivy—and they have been left in the driveway where they fell. The whole house looks off-kilter, kicked to an angle.

"This is it," Case tells the driver, even though she's not totally convinced.

Case glances down to the letter in her hand, the most recent one from Andrea, the one with the specific-vague directions. It's postmarked just over two weeks ago. Case's hand is trembling slightly, causing the paper to flutter. Her gaze snags on one sentence in particular: *I can't wait to see you.*

There are more of Andrea's letters in the duffel bag Case packed for this trip, all tucked into their torn-open envelopes and tied together with a length of gray yarn in a thick bundle. It was important for Case to bring them, to show her friend that she'd read every word of every letter over and over.

The car rolls to a stop, and the front door of the house swings open. A girl appears. She doesn't step out and over the broken steps but, instead, leans against the doorframe. The first thing Case notices is the color of the girl's hair, dark blond, like a bale of hay. It's woven into a long braid and swept over her shoulder. The girl is wearing a denim apron over a light-colored button-up shirt and rolled-up jeans. She's roughly wiping her hands on a once-white, now-grayish-and-stained kitchen towel. She looks weirdly wholesome, like she belongs on a label for something like butter or bleach.

"Oh, there's your friend!" the driver exclaims, clearly relieved. He throws the car into park and then immediately launches outside to grab Case's bag from the trunk.

The girl standing in the door, however, isn't Andrea, and the bland expression on her face isn't friendly. She must be one of the roommates. In her letters, Andrea mentioned she'd been sharing the house with three other kids she'd been at boarding school with, but she only ever described one of them—not this one, though. A different one, the boy.

Imagine my surprise, Drea had written, *when Troy told me his family owned a house in Palo Pinto—just a couple miles from the junior high!*

After taking one last glance at the pictures of the dashboard family, Case climbs out of the car. She takes her bag from the driver's outstretched hand and lifts her gaze to search the house's second-story windows. Andrea could appear any moment, shaken from sleep by the sounds of car doors and the trunk slamming shut. Any moment now, Andrea could be there, grinning and waving.

"Pick you up same time tomorrow?" the driver asks.

"Uh, yeah." Case spins around. She digs into the front pocket of her jeans to pull out two crumpled twenties for tip. "Yes."

She'd paid for the two rides, twenty-four hours apart, in advance—the first from Fort Worth to here, and the second, from here to Fort Worth. Andrea had told Case she could stay at the house, but not for more than a day and a night. Her roommates, she said, wouldn't like anything longer than that.

"I'll be standing right here," Case adds, passing the cash to the driver.

Case waits until the car swings around the curve and disappears down the tree-choked lane before turning back to face the house. Again, she peers up to the second-floor windows. The nail on her pointer finger scratches across the paper she's holding in her still-quaking hand, right across that sentence, *I can't wait to see you.* The stink of burning wood and trash still hangs in the air, but there's a layer of something else now. It's coming straight from the house: the stonelike scent of bread baking.

"I'm here for Drea," Case says. She holds out her letter and steps forward.

The girl in the doorway doesn't respond, but she looks down, frowning when she sees the way Case's hand shakes. Case tries to peer over the girl's shoulder, but can't make out anything except the darkened depths of the house.

"She asked me to come today," Case clarifies.

"Are you Case?" the girl asks.

Case grins, buoyed by the simple joy of having been mentioned. "I am. Yeah."

"Andrea's not here," the girl says flatly. "She's not here right now."

Another girl, slightly younger, maybe thirteen, emerges from around the far side of the house. She's running, holding a wide-brimmed straw hat onto her head with one hand and carrying a wicker basket lined with cloth in the other. When she sees Case, she stops so suddenly she nearly trips over her own feet.

"Is that a letter?" the older girl in the doorway asks. "Like, a letter on paper? Who still writes letters?"

"*Andrea* still writes letters." Case attempts another smile, but this one gets stuck. She extends the envelope out farther. "See? This is her handwriting."

All Case gets in response is the girl's indifferent stare, which makes her feel stupid for even attempting to be cheery. She drops her hand to her side. The envelope slaps against her leg.

"Where did you come from?" the younger girl asks, approaching Case. She also has hair the color of straw, Case notices, as the girl pulls her own braid over her shoulder and starts to tug at its ends.

"Not that far," Case replies. "Fort Worth."

"I like Fort Worth!" The younger girl looks to the doorway. "Kendall, remember when we used to—"

"Steph," the older girl warns. "Stop."

The smell of the baking bread is stronger now, tangy and bright, like sourdough. The older girl—Kendall—lifts her nose to sniff the air. Her expression is still neutral to the point of bored, but Case notices the hard way she grips her dirty towel in her hands, causing her knuckles to pale. There's dough crusted around the girl's nail beds, and dried in spots on her palm and the pad of her thumb.

"You're late." Kendall extends her arm toward the younger girl—Steph. "I need the eggs."

Steph hands over the basket, and Kendall turns, disappearing into the house.

Case listens to the long screech of a cicada—a needle-sharp sound she'll recognize as long as she lives—and then looks helplessly to the younger girl.

"Um . . . hey," Case offers.

Steph smiles, bright and true, like sun on glass.

"It's almost time for breakfast," the girl says. "Come inside if you're hungry."

If Kendall had walked off a label for butter, then the boy sitting across from Case at the kitchen table could be from a billboard for watches or cuff links or cologne. He is too clean. His white shirt is too white. It's not breezy linen, but a cotton button-up pressed into offensively hard angles. The sleeves of that shirt are rolled up, and he has his elbows resting on a wooden table that looks at least a hundred years old. The table is covered in nicks and crumbs, but not the boy. He is . . . Case thinks for a moment. He is *pristine*. Case can smell his soap—a pure white bar.

Just when she thinks she might be staring at him too long, the boy gifts Case with a grin. He tosses a toothpick into his mouth, grinds and swivels it around with his teeth. Case looks away. She hates when people chew on toothpicks.

Kendall is at the kitchen counter rolling out a disc of dough with a wooden pin that looks as old and worn as the table. Right beside where Kendall stands is a metal stove—a squat cast-iron beast of a thing. Over on one of the gas burners, bacon is frying in a skillet, creating a little symphony of meat and grease. Steph is standing next to Kendall at the counter, sorting her eggs into a carton. No one is talking, and Case gets the sense she's entered a scene that plays out the same way every single morning.

But then the boy—the *pristine* boy—pushes a French press across the table toward Case.

"Have some coffee," he says, "before it gets cold."

Case grabs a cup from a stack in the center of the table and pours. The sip she takes is bitter and burns her tongue, but she doesn't hiss or make a face. She may not be able to hide the tremors that often plague her hands, but she's good at hiding her reactions to the things she finds painful or unpleasant.

"You're Troy," Case says, forcing down another sip. "This is your house."

"My family's house, actually." Troy sits back in his chair. "We're from California—Manhattan Beach, near LA." He pauses, as if granting Case time to process that information. "But my grandparents bought this place a few years ago as an investment property."

Case snorts out a laugh before she realizes that wasn't a joke.

"An investment property," Case repeats. "For real? Out *here*?"

"Not so much the house," Troy says. "But the land, yeah."

"You know Drea's originally from just down the road," Case adds. "Me too."

"I know," Troy says. "Small world, right?"

There's a creak above, in the ceiling. Case's gaze snaps up at the sound—a footstep, maybe.

"It's no one," Troy says, as if reading her thoughts. "The house is old. It makes sounds."

"How do you know about Troy?" Steph asks from across the room. "Did Andrea write to you about him?"

Case looks to the girl. She hasn't cleaned up since being outside. An exposed patch of skin at her bare throat is caked with a mix of dirt and sweat. There's a smear of something—mud or chicken shit—across her wrist. Stuck to that smear is the tiniest feather.

"She did, actually," Case replies.

Troy is the roommate Case knows about. He is *the* boy. Case knows, for example, that Drea and Troy met two years ago, when they were sophomores, in fall semester Ethics class. He was *brilliant*, Andrea wrote, knew so much about all kinds of things, but he was also kind and generous. She could hardly believe when, during the first signs of the eruption, Troy had grabbed her by the elbow in the hallway, hustled her out the door and into Abby's car, offering to let her—the scholarship kid from the sticks—tag along with his WASPy gang of friends and stay at his country house, halfway across the state, for the whole spring and summer, maybe even longer if their school reopening was delayed.

In her more recent letters, Andrea mentioned how, on some mornings, she and Troy would wade into the Brazos River together and try half-heartedly to catch fish. When they were alone, ankle-deep in the cold, muddy water, Troy would smile as wide as a sunrise. His green eyes would shine. Andrea said she swore she could feel the riverbed shift.

Case looks into Troy's dark eyes—dark like the water of the river after it hasn't rained for weeks, when it's flat and full of mud, not a flattering shade of green at all. She doesn't see anything magical. For sure, the ground beneath her doesn't move.

"Did Andrea write about *me*?" Kendall asks, slapping her rolling pin against the dough. "Steph, get a dish towel, would you? Drain the bacon."

"She did *not*," Case says. She sets her coffee cup on its saucer with a *clang*. "So. Where's Drea?"

"I've never heard anyone call her that before. *Dray*-ah." Kendall draws out the syllables so that they sound distorted and ugly. She whacks the pin down again and pushes it roughly across the dough, causing the whole counter to shake.

"She went to Millsap, probably," Troy says. "To see her mom. She does that sometimes."

"So she drove?" Case asks. The small town of Millsap is close but not *that* close—at least a couple hours' walk, if not more. "Is there a car here?"

"Only Abby uses the car," Steph says.

Case watches the younger girl peel the strips of cooked bacon from the skillet with her shit-smeared fingers and then press them between two layers of dish towels. When she thinks no one is looking, Steph leans in, rips off a piece of the meat, and pops it into her mouth.

Case thinks: *This girl is sort of wonderful.*

"Abby also lives here," Troy finally offers.

"I gathered that, yeah," Case replies. "Someone came and picked Drea up, then?"

Troy grunts in response and then nudges at the French press again, silently urging Case to refill her cup. She doesn't want to. Not just because it's bad coffee, but because Case is beginning to feel sick. The tremors in her hand are getting worse, and are now starting to ripple into her wrist, to her elbow, to her shoulder and into the cords of her throat, up to the outside corner of her right eye. It always happens so fast: the activation, the escalation. If she doesn't fix this soon, she'll get a headache. It'll start as an annoying throb, then evolve into a glowing crown of pain that will last for hours.

"The thing is, she told me to come today," Case says. "She told me to come *this morning*. I don't know why she'd do that and not be here."

Kendall pauses in her abuse of the dough to open the door of the oven. Using a kitchen towel, she pulls out a loaf of bread and then spins around quickly to plunk it in the middle of the table.

"Wait," she commands, tossing the towel to Troy. "I know you won't, but you should. It's still too hot."

Troy swivels his toothpick in his mouth and, using the same towel Kendall just had in her hands, grabs the bread and breaks it right down the middle. It's still *very* hot. Steam rises from its center. The most glorious smell of yeast and earth and stone hits Case full in the face.

"Are you sure she said today?" Troy asks. He tears off a smaller piece of bread and sets it aside to cool.

Case opens the letter to check, which she doesn't have to do, because she's checked a hundred times. This is the right date, the right time, the right house. She holds up the piece of paper so Troy can read for himself.

"I don't know what to tell you," Troy replies, his eyes still scanning the letter. "You're welcome to wait here as long as you want, though. There's not much to do, but after we eat, you can maybe walk down to the river."

Kendall grunts in disapproval.

"I can show you the paths if you want," Steph offers.

Frustrated, Case pushes back from her seat, crosses the kitchen to where she dropped her duffel, and crouches to search for her phone. Once she finds it, she unlocks the screen and huffs out a breath. Last night, she fell asleep before remembering to connect it to the charger, so now the battery is down to 4 percent. She finds Andrea's name in her old sent messages, fires off a text, then immediately places a call. She lets the phone ring while at the same time listening to the house, trying to locate the twin ring from within. While she listens, Case finds an outlet near the sink and plugs in her phone. The digital pulse in her ear starts to sound increasingly like a fuzzy echo, getting distant, quieter as it rings and rings.

"Calls don't really connect out here," Kendall says.

In her heart, Case knows that's true. It's always been hard to get bars around here. Yes, there are cell towers and satellites, but there are also trees and hills and, lately, low-slung clouds that block signals.

Kendall throws her dough into a large glass bowl, tosses a towel on top, and then slides it to the back of the counter, where it'll rest for a while to rise. She then grabs the plate of drained bacon, a crock of butter, and some honeydew melon that's been sliced into perfect crescents, and pivots to set everything out on the table. She wipes her hands on her apron, clearly so proud of herself, pulls out a chair, and takes a seat.

"Are you nervous?" Kendall asks, as she pours herself a cup of coffee.

Case finally ends the call and turns around.

"You look like you're nervous," Kendall says. "Your hand is shaking."

"That's not why my hand is shaking," Case says. The yellow sliver at the top corner of her phone screen now shows a whopping 11 percent.

"I'm going to the river," she says. Steph makes a move to follow, but Case waves her off. "I'll find the way myself. When Drea gets back, tell her where I went, okay?"

On her way past the table, Case leans over to tear off a piece of the hot bread. Her shoulder bumps Kendall's head.

"That was rude," Kendall mutters.

Case doesn't reply. She hustles out of the kitchen and into the main entryway of the house.

The kitchen was painted pale lemon yellow and punctuated by sad streaks of sun, but the empty entryway is bright gray. Above, there's a skylight embedded in the slanted roof, and, as she passes through, Case looks up to see the quick shadow of a bird flying by. She pushes open the front door, practically running, barely remembering to leap over the broken steps. Outside, the air still stinks like trash.

Clutched in her hand, along with the wedge of hot bread, is a pill that Case managed to snatch from the small medication bottle that was buried alongside her phone and charger in the depths of her duffel bag. Case jogs around the side of the house, tilts her head back to the drab morning clouds, and swallows the tiny round disc dry.

NINE

WHO STILL WRITES LETTERS?

Kendall had asked the question like the very idea was absurd.

All Andrea ever *did* was write—on paper, on her hand, on the inside of her locker, in Word docs, in Google Docs, in notes on her phone, in pencil, in marker, in pen.

Case thinks of Andrea's letters—the ones in her duffel in the kitchen, the ones all stacked up and tied together in a bundle.

Case wrote Andrea back only one time. One letter. And it wasn't particularly heartfelt. Case didn't spill her guts, because she didn't think she was the type of person who had guts to spill. No one had ever described her as *deep*. She was a simple person.

The one letter—Case's letter—was about her new school in Fort Worth and how she'd somehow managed to shed the grimy layer of a country person and successfully blend in with the rest of the city kids. Her grades, combined with her "minority status," combined with her "hardships," were good enough to earn Case a scholarship to the University of Oregon, which she'd chosen in part because it was far, far away from the Brazos River. Her freshman year would start at the end of this month—in just a couple of weeks. Case was thrilled.

And that was pretty much it. That was the extent of Case's letter: half a page written in handwriting she thought looked like it belonged to an unfocused third grader, put in a real envelope and sealed with spit. No stamp, though, because Andrea said mail didn't get delivered out to the house.

And last night, Case had placed her one letter on top of all of Andrea's letters and tied everything together. She was planning on giving them to her friend today, this morning. That plan, however, was already snarled up.

"Drea!" she calls out once she bursts through the tree line and reaches the water's edge. Maybe her friend didn't leave. Maybe she's out here in the woods, a few minutes' walk from the house, waiting to be found. "*Drea!*"

The name soars, bends with the river, bangs against the low clouds.

Barely a river. Lately, more like muddy bank and rock than anything else. The water is a thin rope winding through a shallow valley. In one direction, that rope runs west, toward the scaffolded highway bridge in the far-off distance. In the other direction, it extends a little ways, then bends southward and out of sight.

There's nothing to it—this little trickle. Case can't help but be moved by the sight, though. She spent so much of her childhood in this water. She waded in it, swam in it when the levels were higher, had been thrown into it, had her first kiss and more in it, soaked for hours in it. Even now, she can close her eyes and picture different stretches of it, and what those stretches looked like in all the seasons of the year. On a frosted winter morning, on a spring day in the cool and sparkling sun, and during the wild whipping winds that come before tornadoes. She knows the smells—mostly bright, like fish and sand, though at times, the trash fires and the exhaust from cars on the highway leave a harsh and lingering tang.

Now, after six months' worth of ash in the air, the leaves on some of the trees have prematurely faded from green to sunset yellow. The water level has dropped, drying out the banks, revealing roots of the trees that line it. Case wonders how many fish have died—millions, probably. There are unsightly streaks of black and gray on the banks. But still, barely filled and partially ruined, the river is home.

Strange that all she wanted—*wants*—is to be far away from this place, but now that she's back it feels almost like her bones fit together better in her body.

Case calls out to her friend again, and again gets no reply. She bends into a crouch and grabs a long, sturdy stick to jam in the soft earth to serve as a place marker. She then picks a direction at random—away from the bridge— and starts walking, staying close to the trees and following the curve of water.

In a letter Drea had sent at the beginning of the summer, she told Case about a camp she'd made on the banks, with a woven hammock she was forced to shake out every day because of the spiders and their overnight webs. Drea said she had an Igloo cooler she used for storage—not for food or drinks, but for books and paper, and for a battery-powered lantern she would use in case she got stuck out in the dark. Case wishes she could remember if there were any details in that letter that would help her find her friend's hideaway, like the description of a wiggle in the water or a particularly crooked tree.

As she walks, she scans the woods on this bank and on the far one, looking for something unnatural, even though unnatural things aren't actually that rare. This isn't untouched country. People own this land and have for centuries. And where there are people, there is trash. In a short span of time, Case comes across an abandoned freezer, on its side with its lid gaping open and hanging from only one hinge; the rusted half of an oil drum; a once-yellow Frisbee coated in mold; a pair of sunglasses with one of the lenses missing; at least six sun-bleached aluminum cans; and three discarded aerosol cans.

Through the occasional breaks in the trees and past the hazy clouds, Case can see the hills, including the one the locals call White Sky—the tallest and the widest, the most distant of the distant. There's a story about White Sky, and, of course, Case knows it: A girl, four or five years old, ran off to chase a fox and never came home. For three days, her family searched alongside volunteers from around the county, and on the third morning the girl was found, unharmed, walking barefoot down the sandy north bank of the Brazos. The girl wasn't thirsty. She wasn't hungry. She was wearing a crown of braided ivy in her tangled black hair. She told the police and her parents that an older girl had found her early on and had taken care of her. Together, they'd eaten mint pulled from the ground, figs from a wild tree, and, one night, a rabbit caught with a lucky snare. They'd spent most of their time singing songs, but the little girl couldn't really remember how any of them went—neither the rhythm nor the words—just that in one they sang *'round, 'round, 'round* while holding hands and spinning in a circle as fast as they could until they both dropped, dizzy, to the ground.

When she was asked to describe the older girl, all the little girl could say was that she had very long blond hair—so blond it was almost white—and dark eyes. Then the little girl laughed, in a weird pitch that those who knew her had never heard before.

This story was meant to scare children, and its simple lesson was something like this: There are strangers everywhere. They will find *you* before you find *them*. If they find you, they will change you.

Kids heard the story of the lost girl on White Sky and shuddered, but not Case. As a girl growing up poor in the shadow of these hills, Case had always hoped a stranger would come out of the trees and find her and take her away. She wasn't afraid of change. She *wanted* to be transformed, to become unrecognizable, to be a little queen in a crown of leaves.

All around Case are hills and trees and trash and rocks, but nowhere is there a tidy camp, a hammock strung up between two thick trees, or a lantern sitting atop a cooler full of books and paper. There is no girl thin enough to disappear in that hammock if it weren't for the waves of dark hair that would spill out the sides.

"Drea!" calls Case again, cupping her mouth with her hands.

Again, her voice bounces off the banks. Case waits, peering into the trees and downriver the same way she peered into the dark windows of the house when she first arrived. Never has she wanted to see anyone so badly. What she wouldn't give to snap her fingers and have her friend appear right then and there.

Her fingers. Her fingers have stopped shaking. Just thinking about the pill dissolving into her blood, working its way to her misfiring nerves, makes her shake out her shoulders, makes everything better.

Case stops, is about to turn to head back to the house, when she hears a gunshot. The sound is so loud and close that Case yelps. Her knees give out, and, on instinct, she smacks both palms flat against her ears. Out here, it's hard to tell where a shot is coming from, even when it's close, because of the way the sound echoes off the rocky terrain. Case straightens up and spins around, looking for smoke, puffs of powder rising from a barrel. There's nothing, but that might be because the thick clouds and tree branches have absorbed it all.

"Hello?" Case calls. She waits, then whispers, "Shit."

Case releases a loud breath, then rakes her fingers through her hair, trying to convince herself she was only slightly startled, not truly scared. There are all kinds of reasons people shoot guns out here: target practice, boredom, to kill an invading creature like a rabid dog or a rattlesnake. If a person owns enough acreage, the law says they don't need a reason. On its own, the sound of a shot isn't necessarily anything to fear.

As she makes her way down the bank, though, toward where she left the stick lodged into the mud as a marker, Case's breaths are uneven. She's hustling, fighting the urge to look over her shoulder. She's bracing herself for more shots, but none come. It was just the one—that solitary, echoing boom.

There's no one left in the kitchen when Case returns and tries calling Andrea again. Her phone's charged to 42 percent, but the call she places disconnects right after the first ring. Case unplugs her phone, leaving the charger dangling from the outlet, then hustles outside and down the gravel lane in an attempt to see if she can get more bars outside. She sends Drea a text, which fails to go through, then another, which also fails to go through.

"Oh, come on," she mumbles.

Case stops in the middle of the lane. She knows the number to Andrea's old house in Millsap by heart and starts typing it in. Maybe the roommates were right. Maybe Drea got her days messed up and went home to visit her mom. Finally, Case hears ringing and lets out a squeak of joy. Then she hears something else—fuzzy, like music forcing its way through a bad antenna—and assumes it's coming from behind the house. The music gets louder, and Case puts a hand over her ear to muffle the sound. She drops to a crouch, as if making herself smaller will help her hear better. Case is too full of hope, too distracted by the possibility of a call to Andrea actually connecting, to notice the car that's coming around the bend, heading straight toward her.

What happens next isn't graceful: Case cries out, drops the phone, falls straight down, tries to back away, and is somehow able to kick up her right leg just in time for her foot to not get run over. The heel of her boot thuds awkwardly against the driver's-side door of the car, the rubber of the sole squealing and leaving a long black streak against the white paint. Case's ankle jolts on impact, but she manages to scoot back farther, right into a nest of brambles at the edge of the lane.

She cries out again—in surprise more than pain—and the car stops. The driver's-side door flies open, and a girl jumps out. She's a blur of white: ultra-blond hair, white T-shirt, and white slip-on sneakers, all set against a white car and a sun that's fighting its way toward brightness. From the car radio blares that fuzzy music, a song punctuated by people talking, stations cutting out and overlapping.

"Oh my god," the girl gasps. She doesn't know what to do with her hands. They're opening, closing, then reaching out, then pulling back. "Oh man. Are you okay? I didn't see you—no one's ever out here. I'm so sorry." Again, the girl reaches toward Case. Again, she stops. "Seriously, are you okay? Your shirt's ripped. I think you're bleeding."

Case shifts to a seated position, wincing. Sure enough, there's a long tear in the sleeve of her shirt, starting just above her elbow and extending nearly all the way to the cuff. From what she can see, there are no deep cuts, but her arm is badly rashed from the road. Dots of blood are rising to the surface. Case plucks out a couple of burrs from the skin near her wrist and then presses her hand hard against the fabric, to stem the bleeding and dull the burn.

Facedown in the dirt, a foot or so away, is Case's phone. She reaches for it and picks it up. The glass is splintered, but the screen still works. Even before the phone reaches her ear, Case can hear the digitized female voice telling her that her call can't be completed as dialed. Her heart sinks.

"I'm okay," Case says finally. "I'm okay."

"What are you doing here?" The girl's tone has shifted quickly from worry to flat-out distrust. "Are you with Charlie?"

"Charlie?" Case asks. "No. I was trying to get a signal on my phone—to call Andrea. I'm a friend of hers. My name is Case."

The girl tilts her head, assessing for a moment, like she's

not totally convinced. Eventually, though, she offers Case her hand and helps haul her up to standing.

"Well, hello, Case. I'm Abby. Get in, then." Abby motions toward the still-running car. "I'll drive you the rest of the way—and help clean you up some."

As they approach the house, the fuller morning sun reveals more flaws. The peeling paint on the eaves and shutters look, Case thinks, like book pages stuck midflutter. There's also the severe seesaw tilt of the whole structure. Both Kendall and Troy are outside, waiting. Maybe they heard Case's shouts or the sudden squeal of Abby's brakes. Kendall, again, is leaning against the doorframe, but Troy is out past the broken steps, with his hands in his pockets and another toothpick balanced between his lips.

"Took you a while!" calls Kendall.

"No, it didn't!" shouts Abby through her open window. She kills the engine, climbs out, then immediately spins around to open the back door.

"A little help?" she calls out cheerfully to her roommates, who still haven't moved from their positions.

Troy eventually approaches the car, though it seems like he'd rather not. He's walking superslow, and he keeps his hands in his pockets right up until Abby hands off a bundle of canvas bags stuffed with groceries.

Before Troy turns away, he stops to press a kiss to Abby's temple.

"Aw, missed you." Abby nuzzles Troy briefly, and then

bumps the car door shut with her hip. "Is there still food?" she says. "Kendall, can you make more coffee?"

"No," Kendall replies, straight-faced.

"In case anyone was wondering," Case says, climbing out of the passenger seat and slamming the door shut behind her, "she almost ran me over."

"It was an accident," Abby says to her roommates. "And I apologized."

"But you're okay?" Troy asks, then he turns away before Case can even answer.

In the doorway, Kendall rolls her eyes and heads into the house while Abby and Troy chat on their way across the driveway.

Case is still standing there—not in *pain* pain, but still hurting, especially the one ankle that whacked against the side of Abby's car. A pathetic little feeling starts to settle over her—that she's been run over, torn up, forgotten. But then Abby stops, just before disappearing into the house, and turns to look over her shoulder. Standing against the darkened doorway, Abby has gone completely monochrome. Her clothes and shoes are still nearly bone white, as is her long hair. Her eyes, though, are the color of coal—the same as her mouth when she opens it to speak.

"Come inside," she says. "I said I'd help clean you up."

TEN

THE SCAR ON CASE'S ARM belongs to everyone. When some people see it, they use words like *blessed* and claim that Case is a near saint. They gently touch her gnarled patchwork of skin and tell her that only through pain can someone truly be graced by God. Others treat Case like she's ruined, witchy, a bad omen. She can see the distaste in the hard squints of their eyes, in their hateful, sour-mouthed expressions, and in the way some mothers pull their children away when they get too close.

Then there are the curious creeps. They're the worst. They want details about the fire. What did it sound like? Did it hiss or crackle or moan? Or the smoke. What did it feel like in Case's lungs? Does it still linger on the clothes she had on that night? She kept those clothes, right? What about the damage to her eyes? Are there clouds in her vision all the time? Can she see in the dark, like a bat? Those awful people want to put their fingers on her arm and trace the puckers and whorls. They stand way too close. Their breath gets shallow and thin. Case thinks those people would bite straight into her if she'd allow it.

Abby is none of these types, though. After she hunted through the medicine cabinet in the second-floor bathroom for peroxide, cotton balls, and a tube of Neosporin, she sits across from Case and asks questions—because everyone asks *something*—but her questions don't feel like she's trying to take Case's trauma and force-fit it into some grand-slash-terrible story.

"Does it go up much higher?"

For Abby to dab on the peroxide, Case has had to roll up her sleeve, which exposes the whole length of her forearm and its landscape of scarring. Case clears her throat and shifts awkwardly. She's perched on the narrow edge of a claw-foot tub and is trying to position her arm into the dull streams of sunlight that are pressing through the small ivy-obscured window. Abby is across from her, seated on the closed lid of the toilet.

"All the way," Case replies. "All the way to my shoulder, then back onto the blade some."

"Is it old?" Abby asks.

"From almost three years ago."

Is that old or new? Sometimes Case's scar feels old—old, like *ancient*. Like it existed before even she did.

"Does it still hurt?"

"Sometimes," Case says. "Not too often, though."

That's not true. In general, people don't like to hear about pain—even if they ask, even if they *think* they want to hear about it—so Case has come up with several ways of blurring the reality: *sometimes, sort of, not really.* Her arm does still hurt, though, and every time the pain comes back, fresh and unexpected, Case relives her time in the hospital, when she was raw and skinless and screaming. This is why she keeps a bottle of pills with her wherever she goes.

The doctors said pain like hers is caused from nerve damage, but it's more like nerve annihilation. The nerves aren't damaged. They're missing. Burned up. Gone. Because of that, little sensors in her body are going off all the time, trying to tell her brain that she's in danger.

"It was a house fire," Case offers. "I was asleep when it started."

"Yikes," Abby says. "Were there other people there?"

Abby's question reveals a lot. She doesn't know about the fire. Drea, who was in the house too, must've never mentioned it to her.

"Yeah. But they were all fine."

Abby finishes up with the peroxide, and then hands Case the small Neosporin tube, which is flattened almost to nothing.

"I'll remember to get some more next trip," Abby says, mostly to herself.

"You're the only one who gets to use the car," Case replies. She smooths on the ointment in a couple of quick swipes, though it seems pretty pointless—the second of a two-part process most people do to treat the most minor of injuries—and then rolls down her torn sleeve enough so that it's cuffed just at the wrist.

"Who told you that?" Abby asks.

"Steph."

"Well," Abby says, "it might not be the greatest car, but it's mine. So I'm the one who gets to drive it."

Case screws on the Neosporin tube's tiny cap and then hands it to Abby.

"Since you're the only one with the car, does that mean you dropped Andrea off somewhere today?"

"All I did this morning," Abby says, "was go to the grocery store."

"Do you know where Drea went, then?" Case urges. "Like, why she wouldn't be here when she said she would?"

Abby leans back, reaching over to trace the beads of condensation on the painted-white wall beside her. Even with the window and the door open, everything is a little wet, which is how bathrooms are in most old houses. There's a thin, sparkling sheen on the black-and-white checkered tile floor. Water quietly drips from the sink faucet in a steady *plink-plonk* rhythm.

"I don't know," Abby replies. "How did *you* even get here in the first place?"

"I hired a car."

"So . . . call it back? I can drive you up the road a ways until you get a signal."

"Not yet," Case says. She thinks about the phone in her pocket, and how she needs to plug it in again. "Andrea asked me to come, so I came. I'll wait."

Abby sighs. On the wall, with her pointer finger, she's

started making crosshatches, slanted lines overlapping slanted lines.

"This is going to sound cruel, but we didn't know Andrea had any friends. Aside from us, I mean. We knew she was from around here, sort of, that her mother lived here, but she never really talked about it—her family or her friends. It's nice that you're here, I guess."

"Kendall knew who I was," Case says.

"She did?"

Case nods. "When I got here, she knew my name."

"Okay," Abby says, in a toneless way that Case can't interpret. "Come to think of it, Kendall has sort of an uncanny way of knowing everything about everything, so maybe that shouldn't surprise me."

The two girls are silent. That silence is another thing Case can't interpret. Some silences are tense. Some are awkward, but this silence is simply . . . silent. Other than the dripping faucet, there's no sound—no clicks and whirs of an air conditioner clicking on, no hum of a vent fan.

Case wants to be outside again, where she can tip her head to the sky, run her hands through her hair, and think. Or maybe she just wants to be alone. The urge to be outside and the urge to be alone are the same for her.

"That means you're from around here, too?" Abby finally says.

"Drea and I grew up in neighboring towns." Case shifts on the edge of the tub, putting one foot down to balance better on the toe of her boot. "We ended up going to school together, but I moved away a couple of years ago, around the same time Drea went off to Austin and met you all."

"That's nice," Abby says in her flat tone. Her gaze falls to the tile. "I mean, that's nice you stayed in touch."

"Who is Charlie?" Case asks. "Outside, you asked me if I was with Charlie."

"No one," Abby replies. "Someone from school. He said he might be bringing some people up here to stay with us, is all."

Again, another unreadable silence. Case *could* tell Abby whose house burned down, how Case got left behind, details of her and Andrea's unbreakable friendship, but she chooses not to. Case isn't lying about anything—not yet— but for now she'll be one more secret keeper in a house she's convinced is full of secret keepers.

Not sure of the best way to end this frozen moment, Case does the only thing she can think to do. She coughs.

Abby looks up. Her eyebrows are knitted together like she's confused, like she was yanked out of a daydream.

"Um," Case goes on to say, "do you mind if I use the bathroom?"

"Oh." Abby blinks, and then jumps up. "Of course, yeah. I'll go downstairs. The, uh . . ." Abby flutters her hand, trying to snatch the right word out of the air. "The . . . flusher thing can be a little weird, so you sometimes have to keep it pushed down for an extra second or two. I'm sure you'll figure it out."

Abby ducks out, and Case starts closing the door. At the last second, though, something occurs to her. Case swings the door open and pops her head out into the hallway. Abby is already at the staircase, her hand reaching toward the railing.

"Hey, wait!" Case calls out.

Abby stops, turns.

"Andrea writes me letters sometimes, and in one she mentioned that she had a place in the woods, like a little campsite, where she'd go to read in a hammock. Do you know about that? Like, do you know where that might be?"

"Yeah, actually," Abby replies, cocking her head. "Well, sort of. I think it's on the other side of the river. Her boots were always muddy and wet. It's usually really shallow, so getting across is no big deal. After that, you head toward the south bend, away from the bridge." Abby taps the railing. "I've never been. She's only told me about it, so I'm not sure how far it is, really, or how long you have to walk. I think you can see it from the banks, though."

"After I'm done in here," Case says, "I'm going to go back down there." She pauses. "Do you want to come?"

"Oh, no," Abby says, laughing. "Sorry, but no."

"Abby!" calls Troy from below.

"Coming!" Abby shouts. She takes a step forward, but then turns to Case. "It's no offense to you or anything. I don't really like to go into the woods or to the water. It's kind of scary out there."

There's a beat, and then Abby laughs again—at what,

Case isn't sure. Abby's still laughing as she makes her way down the squeaking staircase.

On the second floor, there is only one hallway, with the bathroom at one end and the staircase at the other. Matching wood doors, stained dark brown, line the corridor on either side. The walls are papered. The main color is a faded pink. The pattern is old-fashioned fleur-de-lis. Case takes a breath and an unsteady step forward. She has to be quick now.

All the doors to the rooms on either side of the hall are open except for one. In the room closest to her on the left are two beds. One is unmade, and the other is made perfectly, with white sheets and a cornflower-blue blanket tucked in almost military-style. On the tidy side, there's also a clothes rack. Chambray shirts hang, evenly spaced from one another, creaseless like the bedsheets. Case bets that if she looks close enough at the fabric she'll see tiny dots of dried dough, which is hard to wash out.

On the other side of the room, clothes—jeans, a pair of overalls with holes in the knees, a couple of wads of red fabric that could be bandannas—are tossed all over the bed and the floor. It's not a total mess, but that's only because a total mess would require more stuff. Aside from the clothes strewn about, the only other things in the room are a hairbrush and a couple of candy wrappers on the bedside table: a mini-mess. Case doesn't have a sister, but she imagines that maybe this is what a room shared by two sisters might look like—difference, clearly demarcated. My side: don't touch anything. Your side: don't touch anything.

Beneath her feet, through the floor, Case can hear the beginnings of a conversation—whispered words volleyed back and forth.

There's no time to listen in. Case moves to another room. It belongs to Troy, obviously. She knows because of the smell: white bar soap. And she knows because of all the bright white shirts on his clothes rack and the two pairs of espadrilles lined up nearby. His window is also obscured by the ivy that covers the house, but not by much. This room has the best view, of the driveway, of the dense trees, and, beyond those trees, the brown snake of the river.

Another room—another girl's room. It may belong to Andrea, but Case doesn't think so. It's been two years since she's seen her friend in the flesh, and a lot can change in two years, Case knows. But this much? Doubtful.

Andrea lived in Millsap, a very small, very rural town at the edge of the county. The handful of ranchers in Millsap had money, but most people had no land, and thus no money. Andrea's mom worked in the high school as a teacher's aide. Out back of the last rental house they lived in, there was a chicken coop. Case remembers Andrea and her mom hanging clothes to dry on their line, the chickens weaving between their legs.

Andrea had a prized possession: a favorite pair of jeans. They were Levi's that used to belong to an older cousin of hers. They were buttery soft, perfect. She jokingly swore that she would be buried in those jeans. She was saving up for a pair of cowboy boots—the nice, flashy kind you'd wear to quinces or sweet sixteen parties. At the time it seemed like a reasonable goal, but now Case knows how long it takes for five dollars earned here and there, selling eggs or doing chores for elderly neighbors, to add up.

What Andrea didn't have was several nice pairs of designer sneakers, *unscuffed*. Or matching pieces of luggage, *monogrammed*. She never, ever carried along with her the scent of powder and biting florals.

This room belongs most certainly to Abby, the strange mix of a girl who seems sort of rebellious but also lets Troy kiss her face and also claims to be afraid of the woods.

There are more sounds from below, through the floor. This time Case stops, holds her breath, and tries to pluck out words. Carefully, quietly, she kneels on the floor and puts her right ear down flat. There's nothing. The talking has stopped. For a moment, she wonders if someone is coming to look for her. She waits but doesn't hear footsteps on the creaky stairs.

Case gets to her feet and pads over to the last room, the one with the closed door. The brass knob wiggles but won't turn. Case squats, attempting to peer through the keyhole. She can't see anything but fuzzy blobs of light and dark.

"Drea," she whispers through the hole.

The whisper is out before Case can really understand why, but then she immediately comes to the conclusion that

Troy—a boy she's known less than three hours—is the type of person who would keep a girl locked in a room. She's basing that belief completely off a snap judgment: his too-clean shirt, the gross way he sucks on his toothpick. But just because a judgment comes quick doesn't mean it's wrong.

Case waits, there by the keyhole, for too long probably, to hear a breath or a tapping or a scratching, anything that could be interpreted as a message or a sign of life. There *are* signs of life everywhere—birds outside in the middle of a noisy conversation, the sound of a squirrel running across the roof, more murmurs now from below—but nothing from a missing friend locked inside a room.

The last thing Case does is go back into the bathroom. This time, she crouches against the black-and-white tiles to peer under the tub, where she finds only dust bunnies and a used Band-Aid. She even lifts the lid of the toilet tank to see if something is hidden in there—in a plastic bag wrapped up inside another plastic bag, taped to the inside of the tank. She knows some people like to stash their drugs that way. Case stole that idea, back when she lived with her mom, stashing not drugs there but money. It's an important place for important things. But in this house, in this toilet, there's nothing.

Case quietly replaces the lid and stares into the water-stained mirror above the sink. It's just midmorning, but already she looks like she's hundreds of years old, like some creature pulled from a bog. Her chin-length black hair is tangled. Her face is dusted with dirt and streaked with sweat. Her shirt is ripped, and little scabs are forming on her arms. She's tired.

The day had started with butterflies in her stomach, but now she's been punched with an immense feeling of helplessness—not like being lost in the woods, because Case likes being lost in the woods, but like floating in a dust storm, weightless and whipped around, without a rope around her waist to anchor her.

When Case finally goes downstairs, she pauses in front of another mirror, this one hanging in the entryway. Directly under that mirror is a narrow table, and on that table is a ring with two keys on it. One of those keys is small and gold. The other is obviously a car key, bigger and black at the top. There's also a trinket: a purple puff, the size of a golf ball.

Case ducks into the kitchen to charge her phone again. Once it's connected, she hears a noise, coming from the back of the house—in the yard. A chair or a table is being dragged across the hard dirt.

"Let me help," she hears Abby say. "What do you need me to do?"

As far as Case can tell, no one replies.

Case quickly crosses the room and kneels at her duffel bag. She's looking for a letter that came from Drea early in June. She finds one with a postmark that matches, yanks it from the stack, and then ducks outside.

Once she's through the trees and far enough down the trail that leads to the river, Case pulls the loose sheets of paper from the envelope and scans the contents.

Dear Case,

Two things to tell you today, and both, strangely, are about feet.

The first: there's something wrong with Gertie's foot. The scales are all puffed up and bulbous. And I know exactly what it is. Leg mites. Parasites.

Do you remember when this happened to our hens? Mom had to dig out a bucket of kerosene and a tin of linseed oil from the shed and wipe down all the perches in the coop. Most of the hens' feet got better, but one had been so bad to begin with that she was permanently disfigured.

We'll have to take a trip to the ranch supply store for the kerosene and the oil, which, unfortunately, I know probably won't happen.

Priorities and all. The budget.

The entire coop needs new fencing. The wire is super-old, and I'm nervous about coyotes. The cost of wire has gone up, however, and Troy is tight with whatever cash we have left.

I've actually never seen a coyote near the henhouse, but I've seen them around in other places, slinking toward the river for a quick drink or even darting across the driveway, right up close to the house. They're bolder now than I remember them being before. A couple of nights ago, one was even back behind the house, chowing down on a mouse. Inside, we were all yelling, flicking the floodlights off and on, banging on the window to try and get it to leave. The coyote just looked up, its muzzle dabbed with blood, and then went back to its meal. The next morning, when I went to look, all that was left was a tiny tail, a pink letter C in the dust.

The second thing about feet: I found some boots in the woods! Not too far from the house. I can't believe I'd never spotted them before. They were just sitting there, behind some rocks, side by side. When I shook them out, there was nothing in them but leaves, a couple of dried-out acorn caps, and a dead caterpillar, a fat one. The caterpillar wouldn't have crawled into a boot on its own, right?

It must've fallen straight down from a tree limb and landed there, in an unlucky place. The soles of the boots were crusted over with dried mud, but other than that, they seemed perfectly fine. I took them back to the house, rinsed them off with the hose, and put them out back to dry. I asked Troy if they looked familiar or if he knew who they might belong to, but he said he didn't know and that I could have them if they fit.

They _do_ fit, and I will wear them every day. They are perfect for crossing rivers.

Love you lots. Hope you can visit before you head off to the other side of the world.

D

ELEVEN

AT THE EDGE OF THE RIVER, Case takes off her boots and her socks. She rolls up her jeans as far as she can, to just below her knee. She shoves her socks into her pockets and wades in, holding her boots slung over one shoulder. The water here is ankle-deep, brown and icky-cool, and she can barely see the bottom because of the clouds of mud swirling around her toes. As she walks, her feet land on stones that are slick with river goo.

Case thinks, *If I slip and face-plant into the muck, I deserve it.*

Back at the house, when Abby said she thought the camp might be across the river because of Drea's ever-present muddy boots, Case *knew* that sounded familiar. She's kicking herself for not remembering before the clue Drea left in her letter.

Case doesn't slip, thankfully, and once she's on the other side, she climbs a not-too-steep incline of rocks that takes her to the tree line.

She pulls on her socks and her boots, stands, rolls down her jeans, and shakes out her shoulders. After walking for a little while, she comes across Andrea's camp. Abby was right. The camp is in the opposite direction from where Case trekked this morning, and she probably wouldn't have seen it unless she'd crossed. It's in a nice, well-chosen spot. The water is wide here, and the trees are old and offer good shade. There's a rock feature on the south side that adds another layer of solitude.

The first thing Case sees is a dull flash of red, which turns out to be the plastic side of a cooler. The hammock is there, but it's clear it hasn't been used lately. One side is still tied to the thick trunk of an oak, but the other has come loose. The sight is . . . disturbing. It's just a limp bunch of pale netting in the woods, already half covered by leaves and dirt, and swarming not with ants or spiders, but with dozens of doodlebugs, squiggling along in their tiny gray armor. Aside from the insects, nothing or no one has been here in a while.

Case stomps over, and the first thing she does is flip open the cooler. There are six things in it: a black gel ink pen; a collection of short stories called *Kiss Me Again, Stranger* by Daphne du Maurier; a battery-powered lantern; a full unopened plastic bottle of water; a small unopened bag of dill-pickle-flavored potato chips; and a nearly full book of matches from a local-famous hamburger place about thirty miles north.

Case is not a detective, but if these are clues, they're not very good ones. She takes the book and flips through it, in case there's a note folded within the pages, but the only thing that falls out is a two-year-old receipt from the Dairy Queen, for a chocolate-dipped ice cream cone. Case smiles.

Andrea lives for that first bite—cracking through the chocolate shell to the soft cream underneath.

"Where are you, girl?" Case asks out loud.

Case folds the receipt, puts it in her pocket alongside the letter, turns to face the river, tips her head back, and closes her eyes. For a while, she stays like that. Then she opens her eyes and stands there a while longer, watching the lazy movement of the river and the birds soaring above and through the still trees.

When she was young, she spent so much time like this, doing nothing except wishing things were different. Case has always loved the river and the sky and the birds, but back then, she imagined herself anywhere but here, usually in a city or on a beach. Now, Case has been to a handful of cities and even a couple of beaches, and she doesn't know what she wants.

That's not true. She wants her friend.

On the chance that Andrea might return to her camp, Case decides to leave the water and the chips in the red cooler—also the book and the lantern. She keeps the matches, though, striking one, letting it flare, and then immediately blowing it out.

She roots around and finds the biggest leaf she can. It's from an oak, brown and crisp. It must've fallen off months ago. Striking another match, Case holds the flame to the top point of the leaf. It burns quickly. The flames reach her fingers, and she quickly drops what's left of the stem, jumps to her feet, and stamps the heel of her boot into the muddy ground below. Then Case kneels, searching through the dirt. She makes sure there's no heat, not even the smallest glowing dot.

There's a noise from the nearby trees. Not a gunshot—something else, something that freaks Case out even more. Sometimes even the smallest mouse or bird can cause a big sound, but this particular noise is so familiar and specific that Case can only picture one thing as its source: a wild hog. It wouldn't make sense for one to be out now—they're nocturnal, and by this time would be bedded down for the day—but Case is convinced that her stomping around has woken one up.

Even though hogs are huge and hideous, they're usually heard before they're seen. Their mouths are loud and wet. They grunt when they breathe. They move like clumsy oafs in packs through the woods, crushing leaves and snapping off branches. That's exactly what Case heard: a grunt and a snap.

Case scans the ground for something to wield as a weapon of defense, and picks up a red rock the size and oblong shape of a sweet potato. She grips it and spins in a semicircle. She's ready to pummel something, but the hog noises have stopped. She waits to hear them again, but not for very long. Within seconds, she's running to the riverbank and repeating the process she completed only a couple minutes before: boots off, socks off, cuffs rolled. She keeps the red rock clutched in one hand as she crosses the slick river.

Once on the other side, Case wrestles her socks onto

her feet and pulls on her boots. She then hustles down the path. She still has her rock, carrying it with her just in case.

As Case nears the house, she hears the sound of a car door slamming, followed by the rev of a weak engine. She breaks into a trot. Abby's car is in the process of pulling away. Case passes Troy, who's standing in the driveway, and goes straight for the passenger side of the car. The door is unlocked. Case flings it open and dives into the seat. Abby doesn't even tap her brakes. She looks over, annoyed, like she was half expecting something like this to happen.

"Did Drea come back yet?" Case asks.

"No," Abby replies. "Is that a brick?"

Case drops the rock on the floorboard. "Are you going somewhere to pick her up? Did she call?"

Abby's silence gives Case her answer.

"Just keep going," Case urges, snapping into her seat belt. "Please."

Abby sniffs. "You smell like the river."

"Please," Case repeats.

Abby glances up to the rearview mirror and the retreating reflection of Troy.

"I'm just going out for some ice," Abby says. She lowers her gaze to the lane ahead and steps on the gas. "Don't get too excited."

The closest town is Millsap, Drea's hometown, which is eight miles away. If things haven't changed in the last few years, and Case doubts they have, Abby is on her way to Timmy's, the only convenience store–slash–gas station in the small town.

Once they're out on the county road, where there is smooth pavement under the tires, as opposed to bumpy gravel, Case slouches in her seat and rolls down her window. It's a relief to be away from the house.

Case can see the line of orange haze creeping in from the south. The air is growing thicker, tingly almost, but Case can still make out the silhouettes of the hills in the distance.

"That hill over there." Case extends her arm out the window, pointing toward the westward horizon line. "The big one—a witch lives there."

Abby hums in response.

"She kidnaps children," Case continues. She wants a response. For some reason she wants to tell Abby about White Sky, about her long-held desire to be captured and changed.

Instead, all Abby says in reply is, "I wouldn't doubt it."

For a while, the two girls say nothing. Abby cranks the air-conditioning all the way up, which seems like overkill. At one point, she reaches out to turn up the volume on the radio, but then turns it right back down. All that's coming in is static. Abby lets out another little hum—this one clearly expressing disappointment—and then settles into her seat.

The car passes big rigs, trucks pulling horse trailers, and billboards for fast-food chicken restaurants and real estate agents. There are also new signs that dot the side of the road, the ones spray-painted with Bible verses or symbols Case can't make sense of. It's precisely these kinds of things—weird hand-lettered signs on the roadside, wild animals becoming more wild, like the coyotes being *bolder* now—that lead Case to believe that six months after the eruption, the world is different, like 30 percent more bizarre or unhinged.

"Why don't you just keep driving?" Case asks. "Go home?"

"I don't really understand the question," Abby says, readjusting her grip on the wheel. "I like it out here. What's not to like?"

Case snorts out a laugh. "But you *don't* like it out here. You told me you don't like to go outside."

"That's *not* what I said. I said I don't like to go to the river. I like to be outside. I go outside all the time."

Case isn't buying it. Because of the way Abby smells—and the way her car smells, the way her room smelled.

Most old cars smell like gasoline and dogs, but this car smells like baby powder and flowers, the same as in Abby's room at the house. The smell is too strong to be soap or shampoo, so it must be perfume, and not the cheap kind that comes from aerosol cans bought from the drugstore with birthday money. The scent must be from expensive perfume Abby puts on every day to stand out from the nature-and-exhaust scent of the country. Case thinks it must remind Abby of someplace completely different, a place she'd much rather be.

"Besides," Abby says, "I'm with Troy, and Troy's here, so . . ."

"And you love the way his green eyes shine in the sunlight?"

The question is out before Case can stop herself, and Abby turns to her, gaping.

"*What*? What the *fuck* was that?"

"Nothing," Case mutters. "Sorry."

"No, for real. What the fuck was that?"

Of course Abby wouldn't let a comment like that slide, get whipped out the window with the wind. Case wouldn't, either.

"It was just something Drea said . . . in one of her letters." Case shifts in her seat. "She kind of likes him, but you probably knew that."

"Everyone *kind of* likes Troy," Abby drawls. "So, yes, I did know that." A moment passes. "And just so *you* know, I'm not taking you anywhere. If you want to get out at Timmy's and go your own way, that's fine. I'm not going to stop you."

That would be great, Case thinks, but then she remembers three things: her phone back in the kitchen at the house, plugged in; her pills in her bag, also still in the kitchen; and her missing friend. She thinks of them in that order, which makes her sad.

"I just want to use the pay phone," Case replies. "Or a landline."

"Do you have quarters?"

Case pats her pocket, even though she knows that the only things in there are the letter from Drea, the Dairy Queen receipt, and the book of matches she found at her friend's little camp.

Abby reaches over the console and pulls down the door to the glove box. There's not much inside: A faded owner's manual for the car, a couple of crumpled envelopes, a few loose scraps of paper. But also, a half-empty paper roll of quarters.

"We use them for when we do laundry in town," Abby says. "Take a couple."

Case pulls out three and holds them in her sweaty palm for the rest of the ride.

This morning, when she was watching the landscape swish by from the back seat of her hired car, Case noticed that most things looked the same as she'd remembered. There were the same stores and abandoned buildings on the feeder, little crosses on the side of the highway to commemorate a life lost in a wreck, faded signs tacked to fences for a politician who had lost his presidential race years ago. But now, Case notices all the signs for yard sales and moving sales.

Once Abby exits the highway and turns onto the two-lane road that leads to Timmy's and the heart of Millsap, Case shifts forward in her seat. Everything is *exactly* how it used to be, in an uncanny way: the Crawfords' place on the left, always the tidiest outside, with a perfectly mowed lawn and wind chimes on the porch that sparkle and spin, but inside is a woman who says terrible things about immigrants. On the right, the little post office with the bulletin board that's probably still advertising hair salons and announcing VA meetings and tae kwon do lessons. The Brewers' place, also on the right, where the sheriff lives with his uncle who was wounded in the Iraq War. Some neighbors came together one summer to build a ramp out front for a wheelchair. Finally, across the tracks, there's Timmy's, still with a sign out front announcing two-for-one cheeseburgers on Tuesdays. Case feels the same way about this town as she does about the river: a mix of wondrous nostalgia, homesickness, and revulsion.

Abby pulls into a parking space at the front of the store, and Case is out like a shot. The pay phone is still there, right by the door. Even better, it's still connected, and the coin slot isn't crammed with old gum.

Case slides one of Abby's quarters into the slot and dials Andrea's home phone. It rings twice, then a woman answers.

"Bueno?"

"Gloria? Señora Soto?" Case thinks she's struck gold when she hears the woman answer in Spanish, but after a long pause, she's not so sure. Out of the corner of her eye, she sees Abby head into the store. "Estoy llamando por Señora Soto. Gloria Soto."

There's another pause. Case deflates.

"No. Lo siento."

The woman isn't Gloria Soto. Yes, she lives in a house just off Old Millsap Road, but she's only been there for a few months. She doesn't know where the former tenant went. She thinks the house was vacant for a long time before she moved in.

Case mumbles her thanks and hangs up. Why wouldn't Drea mention in one of her letters that her mother had moved? Did something happen to Gloria? Troy had said Andrea probably went to visit her mother, which she did occasionally. Troy had *lied*. Andrea's mother isn't even here, hasn't been in her house *for months*.

With another quarter, she tries Andrea's cell number again. Like before, it rings forever—not even connecting to voicemail.

The door to the store opens. Abby paid for the ice inside and now is making her way over to the big metal cooler outside to grab the bag.

"You done?" she asks Case as she passes.

"Not yet." Case hangs up the phone, collects the unsuccessful quarter from the phone, and heads toward the store. "Bathroom."

Abby pauses. "I'm not waiting for you."

"Two minutes!" calls Case, already yanking the door open.

She doesn't make a beeline for the bathroom in the far corner, though, but to the clerk behind the counter, a rough-cut older woman with short orange-dyed curls.

"Excuse me, do you know a woman named Gloria Soto?" Case asks. She can see Abby in the parking lot, tossing the bag of ice into the back of the car. "She used to live off Old Millsap Road? Worked at the high school?"

"No," the clerk replies. "That's not ringing a bell." She looks over to her coworker, a teenage boy Case didn't notice right away because he's up on a step stool, half obscured and restocking the spools of lotto tickets stored over the registers. "Bryan?" the clerk calls to him. "That name sound familiar?"

The boy ducks down. It's Bryan Jennison. A grade or two younger than Case. Basically a stranger in a seen-him-in-the-halls-of-school kind of way. He locks eyes with Case, doesn't even glance at her arm, but Case tugs at the sleeve of her shirt. It's pointless, because a good strip of her scar is exposed through the tear, but it's a habit.

After the fire, Case was local-famous. Her picture was in the big city paper and, for a week or two, on the news. Andrea later told her they liked to post Case's toothy yearbook shot alongside a photo taken in the hospital, where Case was smiling all loopy in her bed, hopped up on drugs and wrapped tight with gauze, along with the caption PRAY FOR CASE.

"No," Bryan replies. "I don't think so."

"Are you from around here, young lady?" the clerk asks. "Is that woman related to you?"

"You're sure?" Case stands on her tiptoes to speak directly to Bryan. "Ms. Soto was an aide. She worked mostly in the library. She's Andrea Soto's mom."

"I remember Andrea," Bryan says. "I know she lived close by, but I haven't seen her in a long time, and I wouldn't recognize her mom. Sorry."

Case grunts in frustration, and again, glances out the door. Abby is leaving. She's backing the car out of the parking space.

"Honey, are you in trouble?" the orange-haired clerk asks, genuinely concerned. It's a fair question. Case can imagine how she looks: torn-up and frazzled. And how she smells: like dried sweat and river water. "You could just stay here with us." The clerk leans over and continues in a whisper: "I can call the sheriff."

Outside, Abby is making a three-point turn to avoid the gas pumps and get to the road. Once Abby shifts the car from reverse into drive, she'll be on her way and Case might not be able to catch her.

Case digs the Dairy Queen receipt from her pocket and snatches a pen from near the register.

"I have to go," she says, scrawling her number, then the address of Troy's house. "Hey. Bryan. I'm Case. Case Lopez."

"I remember you, Case."

"Do you work tomorrow?" she asks. "What time does your shift start?"

"Uh, eight," Bryan says.

"Eight in the morning?" Case sees Abby's car inching out into the road, waiting for a couple of trucks to pass so she can turn. Case scoots the piece of paper with the information across the counter. "Can you call me tomorrow, right when your shift starts? If I don't answer, send the sheriff to that address."

Case doesn't wait for a response. She bolts out the door, nearly colliding with a man on his way in. Abby's car is still paused at the street with its blinker on. Case swerves around a pickup that's backing up to the gas pumps and then breaks into a sprint. Just as Abby's car is about to pull away, Case catches up to it and hits the trunk. Abby hits the brakes, and Case swings around to the passenger side.

"You weren't joking," she says once she's collapsed into the seat. Her right ankle, the one that smacked against Abby's car earlier, twinges.

"Nope," Abby says. "You're pretty fast, though, huh?"

Abby pulls the car out onto the two-lane main road that cuts through Millsap. When they reach the highway, she guns it. The speed limit here is seventy-five, but Abby is pushing ninety. Her little car hardly seems up to the task, the dashboard occasionally rattling under the stress.

Abby tries the radio again, but, still, nothing is coming in.

"Seriously," Case says. "You were going to leave me at a gas station in the middle of nowhere with no money and no phone?"

"You had quarters," Abby says flatly.

Only two left now. When Case took three, she'd had a plan for them all, depending on how much time she had. The first would be for Andrea's mom. The second would be for Andrea. The third, Case was saving for her own mom. Case's mom was last in line because the chances of her picking up were the lowest.

"Do you think maybe Andrea drowned?" Case asks, then cringes at her own question. She knew drowning was a possibility, but she's tried not to fill in the details in her mind. Andrea must have drowned or she was stung or bitten by something. She wouldn't have just walked away into nothing.

"Drowned in *that* river?" Abby retorts. "No way. Even if there wasn't a drought, the river's so shallow and muddy it would be impossible for anyone to get swept away."

Case frowns. "There are snakes in that river."

"I'm sure there are snakes in *every* river," Abby says.

"Water moccasins," Case clarifies. "They're common around here. She could've waded in and got bit."

For a moment, Abby is silent. Then: "I'd believe the snakes before I'd believe she drowned. There *are* things out there. They give me the creeps."

Abby finally slows the car to exit and, after maybe a hundred yards on the feeder, turns onto the long lane that leads to the house.

"I saw you talking to the clerk," she says.

"Yeah." Case sits back. "I gave her directions to the house."

Abby inhales through her nose, quick and sharp. Case swears she can see the color actually disappear from her cheeks. Her already-pale skin goes paler, chalk white. She recovers, though—so quickly that Case can't help but be impressed.

"You told her how to get here?"

"I wrote it on a blank piece of receipt tape—from the register. The same directions Andrea gave me in a letter. I told her to give it to the first state trooper who stopped by."

As the house comes into view, Abby slows the car.

"Are you lying?" she asks.

Case turns in her seat. "Why would I lie? My friend—my friend from *Millsap*—is missing. People from around here might want to know about that."

Abby snickers. "You're lying."

"Nope. Not lying."

Abby pulls the car up to the house and throws it into park. She opens her door partway, but then stops and slams it shut. Case is certain she's about to get chewed out or threatened, told she doesn't understand or she will regret ever having come here. Case waits, bracing for impact.

Something else happens, though. The small porcelain features of Abby's face shift. She was angry, but now she looks . . . serene. Abby glances to the house—to Troy, who has appeared in the doorway as if he has nothing better to do than watch Abby leave and then wait for her to return. He probably *doesn't* have anything better to do than watch Abby leave and wait for her to return, but still. Waiting at the door doesn't come across as romantic, but as something different—something more sinister.

"Then they'll come out here, I guess," Abby says, tipping her head back against the headrest. "Fucking finally."

NOON

CASE IS A GOOD LIAR, and she was forced to become a good liar out of necessity. Her dad—Walter Lopez—was the jealous type. The person he was most jealous of was Case. He thought Case's mother, Mary, spent too much time with their only daughter, their only *child*. He told Mary that Case was spoiled and needed to learn independence, that girls these days were too coddled by their mothers. Walter kept Mary out late at night. Sometimes, without any notice, the two of them would go missing for days. When they came back, usually from a trip to the casinos up north, they'd either be floating on air or slashed by desperation.

Walter bought Mary's clothes, told her what to wear and when to wear them. He made the grocery lists, told her what to cook, told her what to eat. He was in and out of jobs, and he didn't like having Case around the house, so when she was old enough, he sent her out on "errands," which usually meant she had to walk to the library to pick up a book he'd requested but would never actually read—usually a fishing guide or something about restoring old cars—or would make her walk all the way to Timmy's for some snacks.

Case got the point. She started spending a lot of time in the woods with boys, messing around while their parents were at work. She smoked pot a couple of times with friends of friends but could never really get into it. She would then go home and lie about what she did, where she was, who she was with. Not because it was ever that terrible, but because lying was something to do. It was also an experiment. Would Walter or her mother know Case was lying? If they found out, would they care? As it turned out, the second question was moot, because the answer to the first was no.

When Walter finally ran off with a younger woman, Case's mother disintegrated. She couldn't decide what to wear each day, or what or when to eat. She lost her job two weeks before Case was in the fire, and she took her daughter's tragedy as a sign that *now* was the perfect opportunity to start over. A few days after Case was discharged from her long stay at the hospital, Mary took her to Fort Worth to move in with her sister, Case's aunt. Three months later, Case enrolled at a new school.

Things were going okay, seminormal, until one day Mary left. Four days later, she called from Tennessee. She'd met a man online and had gone out to meet him. They were getting married. She wasn't coming back.

Mary said Case would be fine because she'd become so mature, and she—Mary—was a good mother because she'd helped to make her daughter tough and independent, which is just what Walter had wanted.

Case remembers holding the phone in a hand still wrapped with gauze. She was shaking.

"You'll be fine, honey," Mary said. A few seconds passed. "Isn't that right, my strong girl?"

"That's right," Case lied, so smooth.

These days, Case tries not to think about Walter much and how he'd ruined her mother, but there's a memory she can never unshake from her head: Walter sitting on the couch, watching cop shows on TV, a toothpick clamped between his teeth. He yells at Case from across the house, demanding a Coke from the fridge. Then he tells her to go outside and take a walk.

Out back, Troy is sitting at a picnic table that's only barely shaded by the limbs of an oak tree. He has a toothpick in his mouth. On the table is a glass pitcher half filled with water, along with two glasses. Some of the ice Abby brought from the store has been shaken out into a glass bowl lined with a kitchen towel. Troy takes a couple of cubes, drops them into his glass, and then fills the glass with water. He chugs it, then pours a glass for Case, who sits across from him. It's a repeat of this morning—only this time with a pitcher of water instead of a press of coffee.

"Where's my phone?" Case asks. When she returned to the house, she went to check for messages and missed calls, and both her phone and her charger had vanished from the kitchen.

"I don't know," Troy says. "Kendall must've moved it."

Case feels faint. The inside of her mouth is dry. Her breakfast this morning—hours ago—consisted of a granola bar she ate in the car on the way here, a couple of bites of bread swiped from the kitchen table, and a prescription pain pill. She's running on nothing.

"Seriously, have some water." Troy makes a show of sliding the glass across the rough surface of the table.

In movies, this is what happens: A person drinks from a glass offered to her from a tricky stranger, thinking that maybe she's being poisoned. Sometimes, she *is* poisoned. Sometimes, she's not. Always, she's a little nervous.

Case takes the glass and drinks it down in three big gulps.

"More?" Troy asks.

"Please," Case replies.

"There's too many of them." Abby's voice rings out from the other side of the yard. "They'd kill each other if they had the chance."

Case swivels in her seat. What the *hell* is Abby talking about? The blond girl is stretched out in a lounge chair, the kind that would be set up by a swimming pool. This one is set under the limbs of an oak tree a few feet from the picnic table. She's wearing big mirrored sunglasses that make her look like a highway patrol officer. Her white sneakers are kicked off, in the patchy grass beside her.

"It took Steph a while to figure out what to do with them." Abby props herself on her elbow to face both Case and Troy. "We thought they were meant to just stay in the coop until they started pecking each other to death."

"Oh," Case says. "You're talking about the chickens."

"What did you think she was talking about?" Troy says.

"Steph remembers, but she acts like she doesn't," Abby says, flipping over onto her back and then swatting a mosquito on her arm. "She acts like they're all her innocent babies, but they're disgusting. For real, one of them ate another one's foot."

Abby slaps her arm again, then again, then finally reaches down beside her chair, plucks up an aerosol can, and douses herself with bug spray. "The mosquitoes have been really bad lately," she says. "I can't stand it."

"A fortune teller told me I'd die by drowning," Troy says.

Case blinks and spins around. "Wha—?"

"Your arm," he adds, as if that clarifies anything.

"What *about* my arm?"

"Abby said you almost died in a fire," Troy explains. "I'm going to die in the water. We're opposites in that way."

"I think we're opposites in more ways than that."

Abby lets out a snort of laughter just as a door on the back side of the house flies open and Kendall marches out into the yard, holding two large platters, one in each hand. Steph trails behind her, carrying a stack of plates and utensils.

Kendall sets the platters in the middle of the table and then looks pointedly at Case. "You're in my seat."

"Oh, get real," Case drawls.

"Kendall, stop." Troy scoots down to make more room on his side of the bench while he surveys the spread. "This all looks great."

It *does* look great. It's another opportunity for Case to be poisoned, and, once again, she'll take the risk. On one of the platters is a selection of meats and cheeses—at least four kinds of each—all artfully arranged and accompanied by dried cranberries and almonds and tiny little pickles. A fresh loaf of crusty bread is on the other platter, along with a dish of butter with a sprinkling of flaky salt and a small jar of red jam, hand-labeled *Mixed Berry: May*. Lastly, Kendall sets out a bowl of raspberries and a dish of honey that she's been holding in the crook of her arm.

There's a series of sharp whacking sounds coming from where Abby is sitting, and Case turns to see the girl banging the soles of her sneakers against the frame of the lawn chair.

"Ants!" Abby calls out.

"Make sure to eat the berries," Kendall says, sliding in next to Troy. "They're about to go bad."

"I told you that was all they had." Abby pries on her shoes and hops her way over to the table. "You said 'get raspberries,' so I got raspberries. Slide over, Case."

"They're not worth getting if half of them are covered in mold," Kendall says. "That seems obvious."

Abby gives Kendall the stink eye as she plunks herself down, sitting so close to Case that some strands of her long blond hair come to rest on Case's shoulder. Her smell is overwhelming—in addition to her perfume, she reeks of the awful chemicals of a bug spray designed to smell like pine trees. Abby reaches across the table to pluck out a winding slice of prosciutto from one of the platters, and Case can see the remnants of that spray, glossy and floating on the skin of Abby's arm.

Everyone, including Case, dives in and eats for a while in silence. Occasionally, Steph flicks out a tiny piece of bread for a cardinal that's hovering around the table. The little bird leaps forward, snatches up the bread, and scoot-hops back.

"Is Case short for something?" Troy eventually asks.

"Cassandra," Kendall offers, her mouth full of food. "It's short for Cassandra."

"It's not short for anything," Case says. "It's just my name. Also, can I have my phone back?"

"Later," Kendall replies. "It was in my way. I took it upstairs."

Steph is still tossing out bits of bread to the cardinal. Case watches as a much-larger bird, a mottled hawk, dives down from the roof of the house and knocks the smaller bird out of the way so that it can snatch up the bread for itself. It's a strange scene, oddly violent, and everyone at the table stops, momentarily stunned.

"That was weird," Kendall says.

Steph eyes the large bird and frowns as the cardinal darts away into the trees. The hawk seems to stare back at Steph, with its black, depthless eyes, before it flies to the roof.

"So . . . ," Case says. She pops a gooey piece of Brie in her mouth and starts to chew. She's always liked the tacky feeling of grinding that white rind between her molars. "Where are you all from? Andrea said your school had people from all over. I know Troy said he was from LA."

"I'm from Arizona." Abby looks across the table. "Kendall and Steph are from Houston. You're also from Millsap, right?"

"Just outside Millsap," Case says. "My mom moved us to Fort Worth when I was a sophomore."

From the roof, the mottled hawk—the bread thief—screeches, and everyone looks up.

"It wants our scraps," Kendall says.

"It's upset that we're taking so long," Abby adds. "Go away, cruel thing!"

Another bird, the same kind, soars down to land on the lip of the chimney, near enough to the first hawk to make it puff out its feathers in challenge. Little birds like cardinals are cheerful and happy to have a friend, but birds like this are different: solitary and standoffish. Case knows this, and Steph seems to know this, too. The younger girl's frown deepens.

As if they weren't already plagued enough, a red wasp appears and starts hovering over the raspberries. Case looks to the house and sees the sand-colored wedge of a nest stuck in the eaves, partially hidden by the ivy.

A second wasp joins the first, and Abby tries to shoo them away.

"We're under attack," she says.

"That must've made Drea nervous," Case says, pointing up to the eaves. "Why didn't you knock down the nests?"

"What are you talking about?" Abby asks.

Case frowns. "Drea was allergic to wasps. If she got stung, she could die."

"Okay," Abby says. "First I'm hearing of it."

"Are you Mexican?" Kendall asks.

Abby coughs. "Christ, Kendall, that's not what you *ask* people."

Case is still looking at the nest, and at the group of wasps tenderly stepping around the combs. It takes her a moment to realize the question was directed at her. "What?"

"You don't look it," Kendall continues. "Not the way Andrea does."

"Andrea's parents," Case says slowly, "were both born in Guatemala."

"I didn't know that!" exclaims Abby. "Troy, did you know that?"

"I did know that, yeah," Troy replies.

"I knew that, too," Steph offers.

"I was born in a hospital just over in Weatherford," Case says. "So . . . thanks for that, Kendall. Thanks so much."

Kendall presses on. "But, like, where are your parents from?"

"*Texas*," Case says, leaning across the table. "They are from *Texas*."

The noise continues from above, and Case is grateful for the distraction. The second bird now has its wings spread wide and is advancing toward the first while making threatening, guttural clucks.

"Ugh, shut up," Abby mutters.

"Why would you even ask me that?" Case says, eyeing Kendall while at the same time reaching across the table for another piece of cheese.

"Because of Andrea's letters," Troy says. "They're all addressed to Case Lopez."

"Wait, what?" Case pauses with her hand hovering over the platter. "You read my letters? You seriously took letters that were addressed to *me* out of *my* bag and read them?"

Troy looks down to his plate, where he's wiping off a smear of cheese with a crust of bread. "I just saw the envelopes."

"*I* read one," Kendall says.

"You would," Case says. "Because you seem awful."

"Ha!" blurts Abby.

Kendall shrugs. "I just wanted to know who I was dealing with."

"You were dealing with *Andrea*," Case says. Her hand falls hard to the table. "A person you've known for years and have been living with for the past six months. *She* wrote the letters."

"It's hard to really know people," Kendall says. "I mean, you think you know them, because they act one way, but then they do something totally out of the blue and you realize you don't know them at all."

"Wow, Kendall," Abby says. "Deep."

"So did you?" Troy asks, gesturing toward Case's arm.

"Did I . . . what?" Case replies.

"Almost die?" Troy says.

Kendall has been picking through the bowl of raspberries, looking for one that's acceptable. She now stops and waits for Case's response. The girl is trying to play it cool, but Case knows she's one of those people who wants all the worst details, who would eat Case's puckered skin off her bone if she'd let her.

"You all really don't know about this?" Case says.

No one responds.

"It happened at Drea's house," Case says, reaching to tear off a piece of sourdough. "One of her mom's ex-boyfriends set the fire. She broke up with him for cheating on her. He was drunk and pissed, doused gasoline on the front porch and lit it. They only caught him because he was pulled over for swerving and speeding, like, twenty minutes later in Parker County. He reeked of gas, so . . ."

"Oh my god," Steph whispers.

"Andrea doesn't have scars like yours," Kendall says.

"She was in her bedroom," Case replies. "I was asleep on the couch in the living room, which was closer to where the fire started. I never even woke up. Andrea tried to pull me through the living room and out the back door, but her mom came in and carried *her* away. I was left behind."

For a while, no one says anything. People don't know how to respond to such a story, especially since so much time has passed. Sympathy, she's learned, has a short shelf life.

Case imagines that Troy, Kendall, Abby, and Steph are trying to figure out which of the sad details to focus on: the spiteful ex-boyfriend, one friend unable to save another, the burns, the nonstop carousel of surgeries and crying and scarring.

It doesn't really matter to Case, because she's still distracted by the hawks, which she finds more interesting than the fire. Their wings are still spread wide, and they continue to advance toward each other, hopping and hovering. Their talons are raised. They're about to fight, but then, suddenly, they stop. Something has happened, and Case doesn't know what. There wasn't a shift in the wind, because she would've felt that. The hawks, though, they know. It's like there's something secret happening in the woods. The birds take off, one after the other, soaring in the direction of the river.

Steph makes a sound, and Case's gaze snaps down.

"You saw that, right?" Case asks.

Steph nods.

Case reaches for more food but then halts. The platters are nearly picked clean. All that's left are a couple of stray cranberries and a few shreds of fat-streaked meat. Even the wasps have lost interest and have disappeared. There's a smear of Brie on the edge of the platter, and Case is tempted to scrape it off with her fingernail to savor one last bit of salt. She could shovel more cheese, bread, and meat into her mouth for the next hour, she thinks.

Troy reaches into his front shirt pocket for a new toothpick to toss into his mouth, and Kendall takes that as a cue. She stands and starts gathering the platters and smaller plates to take back to the kitchen. Steph helps. Abby sighs, gazing at the dishes being removed from the table, and Case gets the sense that she, too, is mourning the loss of food. Abby then gets up, makes her way across the yard, kicks off her sneakers, and collapses into her lounge chair.

Case is left alone at the table with Troy, and she comes to the immediate conclusion that she's had enough of that for a while. She mutters something about going to the bathroom, stands, and makes her way into the house.

Case is pretty sure Kendall was lying and that she won't find her phone upstairs anywhere, but still, she glances into each of the rooms—at the baseboards, behind desks— but they all look the same as before. There's no phone, no charger anywhere. She reaches Andrea's door, stops, and, just like before, attempts to turn the knob. This time, it gives—so easily that Case wonders if she had imagined it was locked. With a heart beating hard, Case pushes the door open. It swings on silent hinges.

There's nothing here—only a bed made with simple linens, and a desk. All that's on the desk is a cup of pencils and pens. Case walks across the wood floor, bouncing on her toes to try to locate loose boards or hollow spots, where something might be hidden. When she gets closer to the window, she stops, struck by the view: southward, to where the river bends, to the place Case walked through before. Just beyond the tops of the cedars is a dark mass in the middle of the water, black on gray. From this distance, Case thinks it looks a lot like a bundle of snakes warming themselves in the sun on a large, flat rock.

There are snakes in every river, Abby said.

Case doesn't remember if Andrea had a smell—not a smell like perfume, but like her mother's cooking or like grass and live chickens—but this room smells like nothing. Not dusty, not musty, not like vinegar or mothballs. They erased her, or they tried to, but Case knows exactly where to check for signs.

She opens the door to the closet. The small space is empty except for a couple of plastic hangers, but Case goes inside anyway, spins around, stands on her tiptoes and reaches above the door. There, wedged into the frame—in one of Andrea's favorite hiding spots—is an envelope. Case pulls it down and takes it to the bed so she can read in the weak beam of sunlight.

There are only a few pages inside—not letters addressed to anyone, but undated journal entries.

Before Dinner
Troy broke the radio today.
It had never really worked that great, but if we took it out back and put it on the picnic table, sometimes, in the middle of the afternoon, one of two stations might make its way through. Either Christian talk radio from over in Abilene, or the public news station from Dallas.

At first, we all liked to be there, huddled around while Troy messed with the dial to try and tune out static.

Abby was the first to stop listening, just after a couple of days. She said the constant talk about the actual consequences from the eruption (homes destroyed, land destroyed, lives destroyed), coupled with the resulting sense of dread and general awfulness, stressed her out. Maybe a week later, Kendall said she didn't care anymore about the world and would just focus her energy on what she could do for, in, and around the house. That makes sense given what happened to her parents. Around the same time, Steph stopped listening and just spent most of the day with the chickens.

It was just me and Troy after that. For months, every afternoon, we listened to what seemed like the same stories. Statewide, there were ongoing problems with the power grid. Blackouts, brownouts. Because of the random cold snaps brought on by all the ash in the air, farmers were losing their entire harvests. Across Central Texas, people were raiding grocery stores, drugstores, and Amazon warehouses for food and whatever else they might find. Makeshift camps were popping up along I-35. Rural homeowners were fending off trespassers by any means necessary. If things ever go back to normal, the voices on the radio said, it will take a very long time.

Troy seemed okay with this. On most days, he kind of liked the idea of things not going back to normal. He said that if we were careful with the money, we could stay out here at the house for a long time. Through the summer, maybe even until Christmas.

But then, today, there was a story from the public radio station not about Texas, but about California. Wildfires were spreading rapidly, nearing a town in the northern part of the state where Troy's grandparents lived. Evacuations were ordered, but it seemed unlikely that everyone would be able to get out in time. Houses, schools, and other buildings were being destroyed. The death toll was already high. It would rise.

Even before the story was over, Troy had grabbed the radio's antenna, and snapped it in half. Then he threw the radio on the ground, and I watched as the batteries bounced out and rolled away in the dirt.

He looked at me and said that if all news is bad news, then it doesn't serve a purpose. It doesn't help us any.

Right, Andrea? he asked.

But I don't think he's totally right. Bad news *can* sometimes serve a purpose.

Sometimes, it makes me feel less alone.

Of course, I didn't tell him this.

Right, is what I said, because I'm an agreeable coward.

Before Lunch

Abby went to town. She said she would pick me up a couple of new spiral notebooks and a three-pack of ballpoint pens. There's not a lot of paper here, so I have to be sure about what I want to write before I actually write. I keep a lot of words in my head.

I like to talk to myself while I walk down the trails, talk through the lines of my stories, work on things like timing and intonation.

Into*NA*tion.

In*TO*nation.

It's important to make sure the lines sound right coming out of your mouth before committing them to paper. When I'm in the hammock, I talk to the trees, test out the lines of the stories by reciting them up to the leaves. Then, I pause, because sometimes, when the wind blows through and catches just right, the whoosh and rattle of the tree limbs sound a little bit like applause. Then I know I'm onto something good.

I think today will be one of those actual writing days, but I've got to be careful. I haven't *written* written anything out for a while because I'm at the end, and the ending has to be perfect. The main character

71

is processing everything that's happened to her, but not so much that she's _too_ wise. She has to be on the cusp of wisdom. _Cusp_. She has to be fundamentally changed and vulnerable, but we also need to know she can survive once the story ends. It's an important moment.

There's just so much to pack into a person.

It's getting close to lunch now, and I'm thinking about bread.

After Lunch

Listen, I try to stay positive, but sometimes when I wake up in the afternoon after a nap and the sky is red like this, I remember the day everything changed and I wish the world was different. We used to talk non-stop about where we were when it happened. I was having lunch. I couldn't hear anything at first. I could feel it, though. There was a rumble in the ground. _Rumble_ isn't the best word. A _shimmer_ underneath my feet. Like, for real, the ground was shimmering. After what felt like a long time, it stopped. Then came the noise. Boom booms. Like metal screeching. That's not a good description. It was like nothing I'd ever heard before. That's when everyone went outside, and we could see the plumes in the distance, and the rocks shooting off in the sky.

People started screaming. Someone said, _Pilot Knob_. I'd never heard of it before.

The teachers came around and told us to leave the school. To go any direction but south. To call our parents. For those of us who didn't have cars, they would fit as many as possible into the school vans.

We packed our bags, piled into Abby's car, and went north.

For miles and miles, hours and hours, there were people all over the roads.

And I don't just mean people in cars. _People_. People standing on the shoulder, outside of their stalled vehicles, waving empty gas cans. People walking. Entire families. Kids on piggyback. Kids holding teddy bears. Kids holding cat carriers.

Everyone was wearing masks or bandannas on their faces, or had shirts tied around their heads so that the fabric covered their mouths and noses. Everyone was heading any direction but south, just like our teachers had told us. It was so loud. Like the sky was cracking open.

That's still not a good description.

I'd never seen traffic like that. Totally gridlocked. Sometimes, we'd have to kill the engine and just sit. It wasn't night yet, but the sky was black, and there were red lights everywhere. Taillights, brake lights. Red lights trying to break through the haze. Out of that haze, people would materialize and knock on our windows. They wanted us to roll them down so they could ask us for something. I wanted to help, but Troy and Kendall said no. I was sitting in the back seat, in the middle, and whenever I would reach over for the door handle, my hand would get yanked away.

When we were passing through Waco, there was a boy who came out of the dark and approached the car. He knocked on the window, and when no one responded, he hit it harder. He mouthed something, held up something. An empty water bottle, it looked like. We had water. Kendall had thought to pack some plastic bottles, but Troy told us to ignore the boy and demanded that Abby shift the car into drive and swerve onto the shoulder.

The boy knew what we were trying to do. He tried to lunge in front of the car, but he tripped maybe. It was hard to see. There was a thump. The car lurched weirdly, but Abby just gunned it and launched the car down the gravelly shoulder, almost tipping into a ditch. I looked back, but couldn't see the boy. Steph had been quiet all this time, doing that dissociative thing of hers, but then she started crying.

All the time, I think about that boy. I wonder if he's okay.

Abby wasn't able to get me any new notebooks. She said the store was out of them, that they were out of lots of stuff today. She did get me a couple of pencils, though. They'll have to do. I'll make it work.

Case drops the pages into her lap. Drea had written to her about some of this before—the frantic evacuation from school and how it took days for the car to crawl up the interstate—but she'd never mentioned anything like this, like what had happened with this boy. Case remembers Troy's blasé reaction to her nearly being run over by Abby's car. Was it because Troy was used to witnessing people getting plowed over on the road?

Case keeps reading.

Later, Before Dinner

Troy obviously forgot we were all in the same English class two years ago and we were all assigned the same book to read. It was called Death Comes for the Archbishop. *At dinner, he was all worked up, acting like he'd just discovered it for the first time on the shelves in the den, but he was also making the exact same points Father Leahy made in class two years ago.*

Imagine, he said, you come to a strange land.

Imagine: you have no idea what the future holds, but you have faith in something bigger than yourself.

As Troy was talking, the cheese on his plate was warming, getting a little sweaty-looking. I don't like it when people waste food.

Think: How will people remember YOU when you're gone?

I wanted to be like, "Yeah, we already talked about this. TWO YEARS AGO. We know."

Instead, I sighed and took another bite of flaky crust. Kendall made a quiche today, with eggs from the chickens. It was really good. It also had mushrooms in it.

Abby sat across from me, all bored, smashing a blackberry on her plate with the tines of her fork.

Steph was next to me, very still.

Troy was going on about the nobility of the Catholic missionaries and how hard they worked to spread the Good Word among the settlers and Native Americans in the mountain desert.

Nobility. _Please_. I realize we all go to a Catholic school, but he's not even Catholic. _I'm_ Catholic. I've taken Communion, which required not only going to church all the time but also taking a bunch of classes. I had to give very specific answers to very specific questions, asked by priests who were very old and seemed very bored by the whole exercise. Sort of like how Abby is now.

I think Troy was talking so much because of what happened with the radio, and he felt bad/lonely and just wanted to put some words into the air. I wish I could've just gotten up and left. It's usually Kendall, though, who determines when mealtime has ended, and, of course, she was transfixed by Troy.

Kendall. Ugh.

The other day, I found her in the woods, digging through the underbrush with a broken garden hoe. It wasn't the first time I've seen her do something like this. I sort of think she's looking for ingredients so that she can cast spells. Is that a stretch? I don't think so. I never go down to the cellar, but I know she keeps all kinds of stuff down there. Like jams and jellies and potions or whatever.

While Troy talked, I tried to go through some lines from a story I've been working on in my head, without moving my lips, but, unlike Steph, I haven't figured out how to completely disassociate my brain or filter out Troy's voice.

Ultimately . . . , Troy said, beginning some thought.

I hate it when people begin sentences with _ultimately_. I'm _sure_ Father Leahy did that.

Ultimately, the novel is a fragmented allegory about following your convictions and having a vision for a better future.

I froze, staring at Troy.

What was he talking about?

That's not what that book is about <u>at all</u>.

<u>What do YOU think, Andrea?</u> Troy asked.

<u>I think you're right,</u> I said, because of course that's what I said.

Across the table, Abby snorted.

I ended up falling asleep after all and didn't make it to the river. I was hoping to go today while there was a little bit of light. Tomorrow maybe. I think it might rain tonight. I hope it does. It's been a while.

Last month, it snowed for a couple of days straight, but that wasn't all that fun because it was <u>July</u>, and it's not supposed to snow in July. What's even stranger was that the snow was pinkish orange, like the color of a grapefruit. I'm going to try and stop thinking about that.

The first time it really rained out here, it was in the middle of the afternoon, when we were all upstairs asleep. The crack of thunder shook the house, and I heard Abby yelp from her room across the hall. We all ran downstairs, barefoot, and went out back just as the first drops hit the dry ground and bounced back up. Troy was smiling, genuinely ecstatic. He put both his hands out, palms up, like a happy preacher, to catch the rain.

Steph spun in circles while Kendall warned her not to get dizzy. I remember how weird it was that Abby came and clung to <u>me</u>. She pressed her shoulder against mine, reached down, and wound our fingers together. Abby said nothing, but I knew what she was thinking. It was the same thing I was thinking. We were both so thankful for something fresh and new to break the day, to literally punch through the ever-present gloomy sky, something to talk about for the next month or so.

"Hey, remember when it <u>rained</u>?"

Night

Night out here is very loud. The bugs screech, and I can hear the

*baying of coyotes. I pretend that, at night, all the things that are
alive are mad about being alive. Who can really blame them?*

I miss my mom.

It's a nightmare, Case thinks. All of it. But she reads through
the pages again, then again, trying to trap her friend's words
into her memory. Once she's done, she refolds the papers
and slides them back into their envelope. She places the
envelope back into its hiding place.

There are other spots, Case knows, where Andrea likes
to hide her writing. Case crosses the room and pulls out
the chair to the desk, diving beneath so she can see the
underside. There are words here, too: *My name is Andrea
Soto. I'm seventeen years old. I'm a writer. My favorite color is
purple—dark, like eggplant. I'm shy until I get to know you. I
like hip-hop and poetry. I understand Spanish but don't speak
it very well. My favorite foods are pickle-flavored potato chips
and dipped cones from DQ.*

It goes on: this list of biographical details in various
colors of ink. Andrea made a similar list before, underneath
the desk in the living room in her old house, before the fire
took it.

Case lies there for a long time, examining her friend's
handwriting and all the details that make her up but will
never capture her entirely. She traces the words with her
fingers until the tips go numb from the blood draining
away.

"Where are you?" she rasps.

Finally, Case scoots out from under the desk to try to open its three drawers. She pulls out the top one first, then the middle. She's hoping for more paper, pages and pages of it, covered by the words of her friend. There's nothing.

The bottom drawer is stuck, and in order to open it Case has to yank hard, causing something to come loose from the back and drop to the ground. Case stoops down and reaches under the desk, and as soon as her fingers wrap around the small tube, she knows exactly what she's found. An EpiPen. Andrea carried one with her wherever she went, in her purse and in her pocket. It makes sense she'd stash one in a drawer, but if she left the house on her own, it doesn't make sense she'd leave the pen behind. Each one costs hundreds of dollars—a fortune for someone like Andrea.

Case grips the pen and crosses the narrow room to sit on Andrea's bed, but then instantly hauls herself back up to reach for the window above her head. Right after she pushes it open, a grasshopper flies in, as if it were waiting for the chance. It's a big one, maybe two inches long, with a body as bright green as a bottle of Mountain Dew. It lands on Case's shirt, right on one of the front buttons, and stays there. It must've bounced its way up the ivy, because while grasshoppers can soar in arcs tall and wide, they can't jump the height of a second story in just one bounce.

They look at each other, and Case can't help but smile at the sight of the insect's small, perfect face.

"What are we doing here?" she asks it.

Case and Andrea were supposed to leave this county and never come back. Maybe the mountains of Palo Pinto were a dream for some people, but the girls were both convinced this place was out to destroy them. They knew that. They *knew* that.

Drea was halfway across the state, at a boarding school near Austin. She was forced to come back because something terrible happened, and now it's clear that, recently, something else terrible has happened. Case came back to see her friend one last time before moving across the country for college, and now she's stuck in what feels like a horror movie.

Downstairs, she can hear noises coming from the kitchen. Water is running. Cabinets are opening and closing. Glasses are clinking together. Up here, though, Case is alone with a grasshopper; the sad, normal, and disturbing words of her friend; and the burning scent of the country.

ONE

WHEN THE GIRLS WERE BOTH FOURTEEN, Andrea's mom had a boyfriend named Danny. On a clear morning during the summer, he decided to go fishing with a friend and offered to take Andrea and Case along.

The two men found a spot near the pylons of an old bridge, and the girls set out downriver to find a place they could be alone. They walked for maybe five minutes, around a bend and across a rocky stretch of the bank. After crossing the shallow water, they spread out a couple of old bath towels and sat.

Andrea had brought along a backpack with some snacks—a sleeve of cheddar crackers, some gingersnaps in a baggie, and a bundle of red grapes—as well as a couple of cans of Coke she'd swiped from the fridge.

Case remembers it so clearly: the crunch of plastic packaging, little orange crumbs scattered all over her beige towel, the coconut smell of sunscreen, and the cool pop of soda against her teeth. She even remembers what she and Andrea were talking about. It was a wedding.

Not either of *their* weddings, though. Of course not. Danny and Andrea's mom were going to get married. He hadn't proposed yet, but Drea was certain it would happen soon. Danny's part-time job at the paper plant had just turned permanent. Andrea's mom, Gloria, had talked about moving them out of the rental and into a better, bigger house one town over. For the wedding, Andrea would be the maid of honor. Her dress would be a dark rose color, or maybe a shade closer to burgundy, since the ceremony would probably take place in the fall. The fabric would be satin, not tulle, which everyone knows is tacky. The ceremony would take place outside, Drea said. Obviously.

"Obviously," Case echoed.

"I'll ask if you can be a bridesmaid." Drea shooed away a wasp that had been assaulting their picnic since the start and was now hovering close to the open mouths of their soda cans. "I'm sure Mom'll let you."

Case remembers smiling in a distracted, hardly convincing way, then looking down to the grape she was rolling between her fingers. Danny wasn't a creep, but Case knew he wasn't going to stick around. He was younger than Gloria by kind of a lot. And while he technically lived at the house with them, he was out all the time, usually Wednesday through Friday nights. On the weekends when Case stayed over, she could sometimes hear Danny coming home late, bumping around the living room. Then she'd hear Gloria, who'd been waiting up. She never scolded him. She just laughed and spoke in soothing tones. Maybe she'd make him something quick to eat, like eggs, and then they'd disappear into the bedroom.

There wasn't anything really wrong with him, but Case couldn't imagine a guy like Danny wanting to settle down, especially now that he had some extra money to burn.

But that day had been one of those bright and rare days—hot, but not too hot; there was a cool wind; and the air didn't smell like rotten fish or car fumes—and Case didn't want to spoil it with her tendency to steer toward the negative. She let Andrea go on, the way Andrea could go on. That girl could spin the details of an imaginary day like no one else. She'd never grown out of playing make-believe.

In addition to the satin dresses worn on a breezy day, Drea mused, there would be flowers (lilies, tied in neat bundles—nothing too fancy), and, for decoration, little colored squares of fabric knotted to strings that looped from tree branch to tree branch (the fabric would flutter as the wind blew). After the ceremony, they'd eat chicken baked in pastry with asparagus, and the cake would be huge, at least three tiers, with lilies stuck in all the sides. The band would play old country tunes, and everyone would dance the two-step.

"You should have them play 'Amarillo by Morning,'" Case suggested.

"Oh, for sure!" exclaimed Andrea. She grabbed her Coke and took a sip. "For sure."

That's when Andrea turned, and Case saw the wasp, perched at the far edge of her friend's upper lip. Its black wings beat once, and its red body started to curl in on itself. Case gasped, then did the first thing she could think to do. She smacked her friend across the face.

Andrea cried out, and her nearly full Coke flew out of her hand and onto her towel.

"I'm sorry!" Case reached over, but Andrea swatted her away. "There was a wasp!"

Even now, Case has a hard time believing how quickly everything happened. Andrea tried to push off the towel to stand, but she fell over. She might have been trying to talk, but the sounds coming from her throat were high and thin, like when a person blows hard against a blade of grass. Case grabbed Andrea by the shoulders, spun her around, and saw the swelling. The entire right side of Andrea's face, from her eye to her jaw, was puffing up. The skin all the way to her neck was turning purple.

Case didn't know what was happening. She needed to find Danny. Her phone had no service this far away from everything, so Case would have to run. She didn't want to leave Andrea, though. She grabbed her friend by her armpits, hoisted her up, and dragged her a few feet toward the river before they both collapsed. Andrea was still sucking in breaths, but now she was swatting at her throat.

"I'll be back!" cried Case. "Drea, I'll be right back!"

Case broke into a barefooted sprint down the bank, screaming for Danny until she was hoarse. As she crossed the shallow river, small rocks broke the skin on the bottom of her feet. She might've turned an ankle. She kept going. Eventually, she rounded a bend and almost collided with Danny, who had heard her calling out. Together, they turned and ran together, back through the river, back toward Andrea, and Case knew she would never forget Danny's speed, the way his short hair was matted to his forehead with sweat, and the mad look in his eye, like he was genuinely terrified.

When they reached Andrea, she was facing upward, staring at the bald sun, not even shading her eyes from the light. Her chest was rising and falling quickly, out of rhythm, and the only sounds that were coming out of her blue-tinged mouth were small, low hums.

There was another wasp, or maybe the same one, hovering over Andrea's chest. Case roared, reached out, and hit it so hard she could feel its small wings break against her hand.

Danny swept Andrea into his arms and then up and over his shoulder and started running back to the truck. Case found the ground under her feet, and kept Danny's pace as she followed. Together, they hauled Andrea into the pickup and drove her to the nearest clinic, not too far away, where a nurse immediately ran up and punched a shot into Andrea's leg.

And then, somehow, everything was fine. Andrea took one more squeaking breath, but the next one was better. Her purple, swollen face was regaining its normal sand-brown color and oval shape.

"You didn't know she had an allergy?" the nurse asked us. "Really, no one knew?"

Danny had the decency to not hide his embarrassment. He ducked his head and muttered something about not being Andrea's real father.

Case shook her head. She'd known so much about her friend, but not this. She doubted Andrea even knew it herself.

When Andrea's eyes opened, she was looking directly at the fluorescent lights, just like when she was lying on the riverbank, gazing straight at the sun. Case tried to look up too, but the light coming from the long, thin tubes was too blinding. She didn't know how Andrea could bear it.

Later, in the truck, as the three of them drove to Andrea's house, Case became aware of her legs. The long muscles of her thighs were twitching so wildly that she pressed her hands hard against them to try and get them to calm down. The bottoms of her feet were so raw and tender that she couldn't place them flat against the floorboard. She'd run so fast. Before then, she'd had no idea she could do that.

There are footsteps on the stairs. Steph runs by. The grasshopper launches itself off Case's shirt, onto the window ledge, and then out into the ivy. Case hears the bathroom door close. A few moments later, a flush causes the pipes to rattle in the walls. Steph trots back down the hall, but she pauses this time, to look at the spooky shadows crossing the floor, coming in from Andrea's open window. The sky is turning a blurry red orange and will stay this way until the sun sets.

"Hi," Case says.

Steph startles. "What are you doing up here?"

"What happened to Drea's stuff?" Case asks.

Steph takes a tentative step toward the room, but then stops when she reaches the doorframe. "She, uh, didn't really have a lot of stuff to begin with."

"Well, now there's *nothing*," Case snaps, harsh all of a sudden. "Maybe she didn't have much, but she had to have had *something*. Clothes. Shoes. A hairbrush. Where is it?"

Steph glances to the empty hallway, in the direction of the stairs, as if she's looking for one of the other roommates to come and save her.

"If you expect someone to come back," Case says, "you don't get rid of all their things."

"I don't know where she went," Steph whispers, turning to Case. She pulls her braid over her shoulder and starts fiddling with the end. When Case first witnessed this nervous habit, earlier this morning while the girl was holding her basket of chicken eggs, that braid was tidy and new, probably plaited by Kendall. Now, several hours later, it's puffed and frizzy. Her hair is still the color of hay, but Case remembers that hay is just dead grass.

"Did you throw it away?" Case asks.

"*Me?*" gasps Steph.

"You know what I mean. *You.* You *all*. Did you all throw Drea's things away?"

"I didn't touch anything," Steph insists. "I swear. I thought that maybe she went to see her mom."

"No," Case says. "Her mother doesn't live around here anymore."

That actually might not be true—all Case knows is that Gloria doesn't live in the same house anymore. What absolutely *is* true, Case is certain to her very core, is that Andrea did *not* go visit her mom, *wherever* her mom may live.

"So try again, Steph," Case says, bulldozing on. "Tell me how you *didn't* shove all her things into trash bags and then put them out in the bin."

"That didn't happen," Steph says. Then she adds, "There's no trash collection out here."

Well, that shuts Case right up—quite literally. Her mouth is open, ready to fling more accusations, but she closes it and takes a breath.

What Steph said is true. Lots of people this far out in the country don't bother with trash collection. She can't believe she didn't think of it before.

"Of course." Case shifts forward, directly into the red light coming through the window. "If there's no trash collection, that means there's a pit."

Steph doesn't reply.

"You burn all your trash, right?"

Steph nods—a tiny, miserable gesture.

"Show me," Case demands.

Case never would've found it herself. The wide circle of ash and char is in the middle of a small clearing that's obscured by thick stalks of six-foot-tall Johnsongrass. To get here, Steph led Case down the same path that goes to the river, but then, instead of continuing to the water, she took a turn that seemingly led nowhere but into the trees. Soon, however, a narrow footpath emerged, which brought them to this clearing.

"How do you even get stuff out here?" Case asks.

"There's a wheelbarrow," Steph says. "Also buckets."

Most people out in the country just burn brush, but if landowners have enough acreage, they'll burn anything that needs burning. The fires can last hours—days, even—and often leave nothing but a lingering stink and a black circle like this one. Case looks around—to the waving high grass and the nearby trees. Several of the trees are obviously dead, their dry crooked-finger limbs leaning over dangerously close.

"This isn't a good spot," Case says. "All these trees could catch fire. You could burn down half the property."

Steph shrugs. "The pit was here before we were."

Case scoffs. Fine. It's not her problem. These people can burn themselves to the ground if they want to.

Case finds a solid stick and begins poking at the ashes. She's tentative at first. Her swipes barely break through the surface, but soon she starts to dig deeper, prying up larger hunks of wood along with some plum-sized lumps of unidentifiable plastic. Even though the ashes look thoroughly cold and dead, Case keeps her distance, squatting at the edge of the circle.

Steph is watching, so Case tries to keep herself together. It's not going very well. Her nerves aren't humming with pain, so the trembling in her hand must be coming from dread.

"What are you looking for?" Steph asks.

The haze is getting thicker now, practically falling from the sky onto their heads. Steph coughs, pulls a bandanna from her pocket, and holds it up to her nose and mouth. The bad air has always hurt Case's lungs, which were damaged by the fire. She left her bandanna in her bag back at the house, though, and just hopes the haze doesn't get too dense.

"Anything," Case replies. "I'll know when I find it."

It's true, and it's not. Case thinks she made Steph bring her out here only because she wants more evidence of her friend, but what if she finds a faded piece of Levi's denim, a bracelet made from a fishing net, or twisted strands of scorched black hair?

As Case rakes through the ashes, crickets trill all around—from the tall grass, from the trees—and there are snapping sounds from deep in the woods, like when a bird breaks loose a branch, or gravity finally overtakes a dead limb, or an unseen animal wants to make its presence known with a well-placed step.

Whatever happens here with Case, and with Andrea, the woods and the creatures of the woods don't care. Never will.

"The river is rising," Steph says, apropos of nothing. Her voice is slightly muffled from the bandanna.

Case grunts. She doubts that's true. From the looks of things, it hasn't rained out here in a long time. The ground barely gives underfoot, and the grass and fallen leaves are dry. Rivers don't rise for no reason. They're not *actually* controlled by vengeful gods.

"Just since this morning, the water is higher," Steph goes on to say. "And there's a current now."

Case doesn't respond.

"Do you want help?" Steph asks.

"No," Case says. "I don't."

A few moments pass before Steph shoots out another question: "Do you get scared?"

At this, Case stops, turning to look at the girl.

"Like . . . ever?" Case asks.

"No." Steph shakes her head. "That's not what I meant." She gestures to the remains of the burn pile. "Does something like this . . . does it remind you of your fire?"

My fire, Case thinks. She's never thought of it that way before.

"I'm not afraid of fire," Case says, which is true. "I was asleep when it started and unconscious when the firefighters pulled me from it. I don't even remember it happening."

What Case doesn't say is that while she might not be afraid of fire, she *is* afraid of pain, and all of its wild and sneaky forms. Sometimes, it comes on suddenly. Sometimes, it comes on slow. It can be deep and very precise, like a pin-sized stab behind her ear, or it can shimmer across the entire surface of her skin. However it comes, Case is never ready for it.

At this thought, she locates her duffel bag mentally: it's on the floor, in the kitchen, in the house. Then she locates her pills mentally: in their little orange cylinder. There are six of them—five now, since she took one this morning.

"I'm afraid of snakes," Case admits. "And hogs. Have you ever seen any around here?"

"Hogs?" Steph asks.

Case nods.

"I think I've seen their tracks, but not one in the flesh."

"Lucky for you, then."

Case stands, moves a few feet around the blackened perimeter to rake her stick through more soot, and almost immediately something flies up—*springs* up—and Case flinches from the sudden faceful of ash. She rubs the heel of one hand against her eye to attempt to clear her vision, then reaches desperately, bare-handed into the charred earth.

"What is it?" Steph asks. All of a sudden, she's behind Case, up on her tiptoes to get a better look.

Fire destroys almost everything—wood, cloth, small bits of plastic, flesh. Metal, though, is stubborn. And what Case plucks out with her hand is blackened but completely, completely recognizable.

Steph leans in farther, so much so that Case is partially shaded by the wide brim of her hat. "It's a spiral," Case says, holding up the twisted coil. "From a notebook."

In the den, over the fireplace, there's a bust of a stag— what's known as a twelve-point. The same way a tree has limbs, an antler has points. If each antler has six points, then the animal, in total, has twelve. Each point is an indicator of maturity. The more points, the older the animal.

The more points, the prouder a hunter is of his kill. This kill would've made someone very proud.

Below the bust of the stag, and a little off to the side, is Troy. He's standing on a chair with his back facing the room, scanning bookshelves, looking for something specific. He doesn't know Case is behind him, which gives her time to study the stag's head. She focuses on its nose, wondering how it somehow still appears moist, and then she shifts her eyes to meet its indifferent glass stare.

"Do you hunt?" Case finally asks.

Troy's hand hovers in front of the spine of one of the books. He then drops that hand to his side.

"No," he says, turning and hopping down from the chair. "I mean, not really. I've hunt*ed* before, but I wouldn't call myself a hunt*er*. My brother is more into it." He pauses. "Do you hunt? Isn't that what people do when they grow up in the country?"

"I can shoot a little," Case replies.

Soda cans off fence posts, mostly, with a .22-caliber rifle. Once, a rattlesnake. It wasn't threatening her—just sunning itself on a rock. She didn't want to, but she did it anyway. Walter had once told her to shoot any rattler she saw. She was sad about that unnecessary death for weeks.

"I don't really like to, though," she says.

Troy looks up at the stag. "I don't know who did that. It probably came with the house."

That reminds Case: "You said your grandparents bought this place as an investment property, but what does that mean? An investment in what? There's no grassland here, so you can't raise cattle. I haven't seen any evidence of crops."

"Water," Troy says. "There's over eighty acres to this property, most of which is overgrown and undeveloped. But we own land on both sides of the river."

"So you own . . . the river?"

"We own a section of the river, and also down south a little, where several tributaries feed in."

"And that's worth a lot?" Case asks.

Troy steps forward, and from the expression on his face, Case thinks he might be amused. At . . . *what*? Her question? *Her*? It's probably her, yeah.

More than likely, Case looks and smells like she's literally crawled out of the river. She's sweat-streaked, scratched-up, and, now, coated with soot. She can feel it, the grit resting on top of the skin of her hands and her throat. A bead of sweat is actively running from her dirty hairline to the edge of her lip. She tastes both salt and ash.

"Soon, water will be more valuable than land," Troy explains. "Around here, it already is."

Case has to take Troy's word for it. Her family has never owned property. Like Andrea's family, they'd been renters and hadn't had any acreage. She can't legally claim any of the land in Palo Pinto County, and yet she's certain that it belongs more to her than it belongs to someone like Troy.

One of Case's earliest memories was digging worms out of the rust-red dirt. Another involved running barefoot across the backyard to get to her house so her mom could hose fire ants off her feet. More times than she could count, she'd collected fallen tree limbs in a squeaky wheelbarrow and clumsily hauled them to someone's fire pit or burn pile. She has watched painted sunset after painted sunset after painted sunset. She's pried up rocks for no other reason than to see if any multilegged thing lived underneath.

Troy's family, on the other hand, wasn't from here. As a boy, Troy didn't play in this red dirt. He didn't grow up in the shadow of White Sky, wasn't either terrorized or mesmerized by the story of its witch. Case doesn't know what Troy did as a boy, and if she's honest, she doesn't care. What she does care about, and what makes her absolutely furious, is that his family came out here, bought a section of her river and an awful house in which he could pretend to be a proud little king.

Troy reminds Case of all the junk she'd seen earlier, lining the banks of the river: ugly, out of place, yet frustratingly permanent.

"What's in your hand?" Troy asks.

"Oh, this?" Case holds up the coil, twirls it in her fingers. "This is what's left of Andrea's notebook after you burned it."

"I didn't burn it," Troy says, scoffing at the suggestion. "*She* probably burned it."

Case pauses. "She wouldn't have done that."

"Yes," Troy says. "She would've. She liked some of her stories more than others. Sometimes she'd get frustrated, go out, throw a bunch of paper in the burn pile, and start over new."

Case doesn't know what to say. She never knew Andrea to destroy the things she'd written. It doesn't seem like something her friend would do, but it doesn't seem completely outside the realm of possibility, either.

"That"—Troy points to the spiral in Case's hand—"could be months old."

"Her room," Case says, "is empty. Cleaned out."

"We told you," Troy says. "She left."

"She wouldn't have taken *everything* if she was just going down the road to visit her mom."

It's so hard, but Case holds her cards—doesn't mention the journal entries she found that chronicled a miserable existence, or the EpiPen that's currently wedged inside her boot, or the fact that she couldn't reach Andrea's mom on the phone when she called from the store.

"She wouldn't have told me to come," Case repeats for what feels like the hundredth time today, "and not be here."

Troy is standing a foot, maybe two, away from Case—staring at her with those black-pool eyes of his. Case is the taller of the two. By maybe only an inch, but that small difference makes her feel like a giant. She could crush him. She *should* crush him. She could throw him in the river. Leave him to the snakes and the wasps and the hogs. Furious young women like her are capable of some murderous shit.

This, though, is the moment Abby chooses to innocently enter the scene, coming into the room from the kitchen, eating a banana. She knows she's interrupted something, because she stops, midbite, looks at Troy, then looks at Case, then takes a slight step back before realizing she can't just dissolve through the walls.

"Oh," she says, chewing. "Hey."

Abby's eyes widen as she examines Case: fingernails, face, shirt, the front of her jeans. Everything is filthy, streaked with ash.

"I found the burn pile," Case says.

"Okay," Abby says, taking another bite of her banana. "Well. Do you maybe want to use the bathtub or something?"

"I . . . ," Case starts. "Uh . . ."

Abby strides over, linking arms with Case. Case is so caught off guard that she instinctively tries to yank herself away. She is disgusting. Abby is clean. Case doesn't want to smudge up all of Abby's cleanliness, but Abby won't take no for an answer. The girl resists Case's resistance, pulls Case closer, and doesn't seem to care as dark ash transfers onto the sleeve of her white T-shirt.

"You can also borrow some fresh clothes," Abby says. "By the way . . ." With her free, nonbanana hand, Abby points to a side table, and there's Case's phone, wrapped in its charger cord, unplugged.

Case lunges for it. When the screen blinks to life, Case sees that the battery has again drained to single digits and that a text has come in. Not from Drea, but from an unknown number: *Case, it's Bryan. From Timmy's. You ok?*

Case laughs out loud.

TWO

TAKE A WARM BATH.

This was something Case's counselor—the first of four—had suggested.

Case started talking to a counselor a few months after the house fire, after she and her mom had moved to Fort Worth, when all of her surgeries were making her feel as if she were being peeled apart like a piece of fruit. Like she'd told Steph, Case wasn't afraid of fire, but she was afraid of the pain that could appear at any moment, in any place: at her desk during fifth-period history, during her morning shower, during a trip to the mall, during a car trip with her aunt to grab a drive-thru soda.

Case had begun to act out. She smashed a plate on the counter instead of having to clean crumbs and butter smears from its surface. During math class, she tore out all the pages from her notebook, just to see the mess she could make and what the teacher would do about it.

What was making Case so angry, according to her first counselor, was her fear. But Case shouldn't have been angry. She should've been *grateful*. She was a survivor. That's right, *right*? That's what people told her.

Her anger swelled. It pulsed like a living thing. She was angry about being angry.

Insecure is another word Case's first counselor used a lot. Anger was, according to the counselor, a "masking emotion" for insecurity. Case didn't really know what that meant, but she didn't like the sound of it.

The counselor told Case to try and carve out time every day to do something relaxing, time when she could focus on herself and her breathing. She suggested taking baths or going on walks or stretching or writing letters.

So Case took baths, sometimes two a day. At first, they didn't work.

One day, Case failed a quiz in history, and at home, when her mother asked what was wrong, Case hit her in the face with a textbook. A couple of weeks later, Case's mom went to Tennessee, called to tell Case that she was strong, and never came back.

Case, with her aunt and her younger cousin, moved again, but not far, to an apartment just north of the interstate, more toward the center of the city.

There were still more surgeries, and Case was still angry, but the move had somehow helped. She started seeing a new counselor, who never used the words *insecurity* or *insecure*, and she appreciated that. She took baths nearly every night, in the slice of time between dinner and doing her homework, with the door to the bathroom cracked so she could hear the television in the living room. Her aunt liked to watch the channel that played nothing but old game shows back-to-back. Case was soothed by the sound of it all: the dings, beeps, blips, cheers.

Case started at her new school, and eventually the anger went away—or it changed into something else. It dissolved into the bathwater, was shuttled down the drain. Case stopped seeing her counselor.

She's normal now.

Case soaks in the tub for so long that the once-warm water cools almost completely, but it feels perfect after a morning full of dust and dirty water. She extends a wet finger, swiping patterns on the tiles and tracing the grout between the squares. There are dots of mold embedded all over, but it's obvious that someone tries to keep this room clean, probably by scrubbing with a toothbrush dipped in bleach. That someone is probably Kendall.

Case reaches for her phone, which she left on the tiles by the tub, and finally responds to Bryan's text from earlier.

I'm okay for now, Case types out. *I'll let you know if I need anything.* She pauses, then adds *Thanks*, because she supposes that's the normal thing to do.

The message fails to go through the first time but, miraculously, goes through on her second effort.

Bryan's response is almost immediate: a thumbs-up.

Case sends another text to Drea and then puts her phone back down.

For a long time, the house is quiet, but after a while, someone starts moving around. Case can hear the creak of a bed and the squeak of floorboards as feet hit wood. Someone will probably need the bathroom soon, but Case can't find the motivation to do anything but pick at the tiles. Her finger trails upward, almost over the level of her head, when the edge of her nail catches on something. A whole tile loosens and then falls off the wall, landing neatly into her palm.

Case shifts in the water to look behind her. There, where the tile was, is a deep pocket dug out of the crumbly mortar, and in that pocket are several sheets of paper, rolled up and shoved in. Case gets closer and sees swirls of colored ink and, she thinks, so-familiar handwriting.

"Hey." The doorknob rattles. "I need to go."

Case startles at the sound of Abby's voice and nearly drops the tile.

The door opens a crack, but it's caught by the chain Case fastened before she got in the tub.

"There's just the one bathroom here," Abby says. "We never lock the door."

"Just a second," Case says. "Just, uh . . . give me a second."

Case manages to slip the tile back into place, then stands, bracing one slippery hand against the wall to reach for a towel that's hung on a hook on the door.

"I need to go," Abby says. "Just let me in."

"Okay. Okay."

Case reaches for the bolt. Her fingers have barely left the chain before the door flies open. With a yelp, Case drops the towel onto the floor. She plunges into the water and yanks at the clear plastic curtain to bring it more fully around the tub.

Without even glancing at Case, Abby rushes for the toilet. There's not an instant of hesitation, not even the briefest of pauses to indicate that Abby is modest or embarrassed. Within seconds, Case hears the rough sound of pee hitting water.

She sinks deeper into the tub and sets her gaze in front of her, on the mineral-stained silver knob for the hot water, then over to the top curve of her left big toe, which is poking out from the bath. She'll look anywhere but in Abby's direction.

"We're used to each other here," Abby says.

"Sure," Case mutters.

Abby finishes up, fumbles with the toilet paper, and flushes. Case works up her nerve and shifts her gaze, peering through the cloudy-clear curtain. She watches as Abby shimmies her narrow hips to get her shorts back up, and washes her hands. Then, instead of leaving, she closes the lid of the toilet, and sits again, crossing her legs.

"Did Andrea feel bad?" Abby asks.

A moment passes.

"Bad about what?" Case replies.

"When she couldn't save you. Did she feel bad about that?"

"I don't think so. I mean, she did *try*."

"But you don't know that, right? You were unconscious. You don't know what really happened."

Finally, Case pulls the curtain back and sees Abby there, chewing on the edge of her thumbnail. She's wearing the same white T-shirt from earlier, the one that Case dirtied up with her dirtiness.

"I'm sorry I said that," Abby blurts, yanking her nail from between her teeth and shoving her whole hand underneath her butt. "I just keep thinking about it. Like, if this place was on fire, Kendall would save Steph . . . or Troy. Steph would save Kendall. I would save Troy."

"Troy would save you," Case offers.

Abby cocks her head and looks at Case like she's the biggest idiot in the world.

"Troy would save *himself*," she says. "But I also think the point of saving someone is to actually *save* them. If I were Andrea, I'd have a hard time forgiving myself for not getting the job done."

"She *tried*," Case repeats. "I'm grateful that she tried. She knows I'm grateful, and I've never blamed her or made her feel bad about it."

Abby turns her gaze away, out the small window and into the glowing-orange woods, which screeches with the sound of cicadas. The bath Case thought was perfectly cool has turned uncomfortable, and it's sticky against her skin. When she looks to the water, all she can focus on are small islands of soap and grime that float on the surface.

"Did you just graduate?" Abby asks.

Case nods.

"So, what are you doing now?"

"I'm going to Oregon," Case says. "I got a scholarship. What about you? What are you doing in the fall?"

"We're staying here. Troy got into one of the UTs, but he deferred. I didn't accept any offer of admission. Neither did Kendall." Abby pauses. "You asked earlier why we don't leave here. I don't want to leave, because I don't want to *do* anything. These last few months have been so heinous. If someone's going to let me live in their house and not have to do anything—not have to scroll through the news on my phone, or write a paper, or set an alarm clock, then I'm going to do that. You probably think that makes me spoiled, but . . ."

Not *spoiled*, Case thinks. Not quite. The word that comes to mind is *convenient*. Like, how *convenient* it is to be able to vanish into the woods and do nothing.

"I'm not in any position to judge," Case says, tapping her finger on the surface of the dirty water.

But of course she wants to judge—of course, she *does* judge. All day, Case has seen nothing but bad actors stuck in a bad scene in a bad house.

"I knew who you were," Abby says. "I took Andrea's letters to town to get mailed, bought stamps for her."

"That's . . . nice of you."

Abby looks back to Case and smirks. "I thought you were her boyfriend. Because of your name . . ." As Abby recrosses her legs, her foot brushes against the small pile of Case's filthy clothes.

"She loved Troy," Case says, echoing what she'd said earlier in the car.

Abby sniffs. "Troy loves to watch us all fight over him. You need a new shirt. You can borrow one of mine. Or just keep it. It doesn't matter."

"Okay," Case replies. Her gaze is fixed on Abby's big toenail, painted pastel pink, as it grazes Case's dirty shirt, wadded up on the tiles. "If you think it'll fit. Thanks."

"No problem." Abby finally stands. "I'll be in my room."

Abby walks out of the bathroom, leaving the door wide open. She was there, then she wasn't—in and out like a disturbing phantom.

Case moves silently through the water, reaches over with a wet hand, and pushes the door closed with a quiet *snick*. She steps out, dries off quickly with her borrowed towel, tugs on her old underwear, jeans, and bra, and then, after one quick glance to the door, turns her attention back to the tub. She reaches through the dirty water and pulls the stopper from the drain. The slurps and sucks from the old tub are loud enough to cover the soft sounds of a tile being pulled from the wall and papers sliding from their hiding place.

It would take too long to unroll and read through them now, but Case peels a few of the sheets back enough to confirm what she'd originally thought: it's Andrea's writing.

More journal entries. Some of the pages are full of words, but others contain just a paragraph or a couple of lines. It's a clever hiding spot, in a place Case would have never thought to look.

Case waits until the water has almost drained, until the pipes have swallowed the last inch of water. Then she folds the collection of papers in half, and then in half again. It's a bulky wad now, but she jams it into her pocket anyway.

She carefully replaces the tile, scoops her old chambray shirt from the floor, and flings open the door. Abby is standing in her doorway, only a few feet away. Her gaze goes right to the center of Case's exposed chest, lingers there, and then travels back up to Case's eyes.

"Do you really think there's a witch?" Abby asks. "Over on that hill?"

"I'd like to think so," Case replies, raising an eyebrow. "Yeah."

"Well," she says, "come on, then."

With the cool water still sparkling on the bare skin of her shoulders and stomach, Case walks into Abby's floral-scented room. Even after a bath, she feels like she's going to dirty things up again. Abby already has a shirt picked out for Case and tells her to drop her old one on the floor. Then she says she's going downstairs.

Case does what she's told: after changing into Abby's shirt, she drops hers on the floor. Eventually, someone will pick it up, bundle it with the rest of the trash, take it out to the pit, and burn it until it's nothing.

THREE

CASE IS ON HER BACK, on the floor of Andrea's room, wearing a borrowed light blue long-sleeve shirt that's slightly too small. She's writing in black marker on the underside of the desk. Andrea's multicolored writing takes up most of the space, but Case has found a three-by-three-inch square off to the right—there's enough blankness there for what she wants to say.

Remember the time, she writes. The marker blurs at the edges, seeping into the grain of the wood.

Case pauses, trying to distill the story of the last time she set foot in Palo Pinto County, which was also the last time she saw Andrea.

It was in October, a Friday afternoon. Andrea didn't have a driver's license, but she'd borrowed a truck from a friend of her mom's and drove out to pick up Case from her aunt's place in Fort Worth. From there, they went to a football game. This was a big-time, bright-lights rural Texas high school stadium, and the two girls had barely made it across the crowded parking lot before Case started to feel the weight of everyone's eyes. Even though it was too hot for it, Case had worn a jean jacket, but people still stared as if they could see straight through the denim.

Underneath that jacket, Case's scars were still new, still in the process of forming and re-forming: scars layered on scars. Their colors were awful, not the tone of any skin, but blueish and, in some places, darkening toward the color of an old, blown-out tattoo.

Aside from the scars on the surface, there was damage beneath. The nerves and muscles that hadn't been harmed by the fire had been, over the last few months, hacked up by surgeons. Her arm didn't feel like her arm. It wouldn't move the way she wanted it to. It hung limp, lower and longer than the other. The arm-brain connection had been severed. She felt sewn together by sloppy stitchwork. She was sure everyone could see her monstrousness.

But Andrea was trying to make Case feel less monstrous, because she'd always been good at that. From the concession stand, she bought nachos they could share, a bag of Twizzlers, a giant Diet Coke. Andrea found them a spot high on the bleachers, away from most of the crowd, and made sure they sat so close the whole length of their thighs pressed together. Every once in a while, friends came by to ask how they both were doing. Andrea had been at the private boarding school outside Austin for almost a year, and Case had been in Fort Worth since the previous January.

"You cut your hair!" former friends said to Case. They had to shout over the announcer's voice, which boomed and echoed from the stadium speakers. "We barely recognized you!"

"We miss you!" they said to Drea. "I saw your mom at the store the other day. Why don't you come home to visit more?"

At one point, when it was just the two of them, Andrea shifted so she could rest her chin on Case's shoulder. Case watched the players on the field, and she could feel the movement of Andrea's jaw as she chewed sticky red candy between her teeth. The moment *did* make Case feel less broken, but she couldn't help, every so often, tugging on the sleeve of her jacket, pulling it as far down her wrist as she could. She'd taken an extra pain pill in the truck, which she shouldn't have done. The pill, along with the soda, along with the candy and the salty nachos, was making her feel light-headed, a little tripped-out.

It wasn't until the end of the second quarter when a girl came up to her and asked if she could see Case's arm. It had to have been on a dare. Right? Why else would someone be so ballsy, so stone-cold?

Case didn't know the girl. She seemed younger. It's possible she was still in junior high. Also, the girl could've been a little tipsy. She was sipping from a thermos, and everyone knows a thermos brought to a football game is filled with anything but coffee.

Andrea, though—she knew the girl.

"Go away, Betty," she said, ripping a Twizzler with her teeth. "You're blocking my view."

Betty didn't go away. Case tried to look at her, but she couldn't see her face very well. She was backlit by the stadium lights. Case had to tilt her head up and squint. Her eyes burned, and the girl melted into a dark blur.

"I heard it's, like, real bad," Betty said.

Then she reached out—actually reached toward the cuff of Case's jacket as if to peel the sleeve back—and Case reacted by whipping away her arm. It knocked into the thermos in the girl's hand, which flew up and hit Betty in the face, causing her to lose her balance. The girl fell backward on the metal stadium seats, going down, down, thump-thumping against the bleachers on the way, until her foot got caught on something and she bucked to a stop.

Andrea and Case were already up, stomping down the bleachers toward where Betty lay splayed. Her long black hair covered most of her face, so it was impossible to tell if she was knocked out or bleeding. It was also impossible to hear if the girl was crying or moaning, or even screaming, because, right then, the home team scored a last-second touchdown on a third down, and the stadium erupted.

Betty's friends materialized out of nowhere. The ones who weren't flocking toward their friend were descending on Case, calling her a "fucking psychopath," telling her they were calling the cops. Drea shouted that Betty started it, that she should've known better, that she was drunk, and that everyone knows you don't go touching people you don't know without their permission.

Betty was fine, basically. Within moments, she was awkwardly pushing herself onto her elbows, brushing her hair out of her face. There was blood on her bottom lip, probably from where the thermos hit it or where she bit it with her teeth during her fall. Even her foot, which had been wedged underneath the bleachers, seemed okay, only a little scraped up. When Betty was finally led away by her friends, she didn't even limp going down the steep stairs.

"Are you okay?" Andrea asked, once the girl was out of sight.

Case just nodded.

"You want to go?"

Case nodded again.

They left the game right then, during the halftime rush to the concession stand, and spent most of the night driving around farm roads in Andrea's borrowed truck. They slept for maybe three hours, side by side, on the pullout sofa in the living room of Andrea's mom's house on Old Millsap Road, and then, early the next morning, Andrea drove Case back to her aunt's apartment.

Of course, Case hadn't intended for Betty to tumble down the bleachers, but as she watched it happen—watched the girl literally bounce across concrete and metal—she wasn't scared. And she wasn't even sorry. On the ride home, she played the event over and over again in her head. First, there was Betty's question, then Betty's blurred face, then Betty's hand extending toward Case, then the thermos flying, then Betty falling, then Betty stopping. In that short moment between Betty stopping and Betty sitting up to push the hair away from her bloody mouth, something important had happened, and it took Case a while to figure out what.

Later that day, Andrea sent Case a text: *It's okay to feel bad about what happened, but remember it's not your fault!!*

Case read Drea's message with a grimace and responded with a blowing-a-kiss emoji. Then she put on her shoes, went outside, and took a walk.

This is a long story to tell, and since Case only has a small square on the underside of a desk, all she writes is this: *Remember the time when Betty fell down the bleachers? I was disappointed when she got back up.*

She puts the marker down, pulls Andrea's pages from her back pocket, and starts reading.

Later, Before Dinner
A stranger came today.

I guess it was bound to happen sometime.

He's older than us, but not by much. He looks like he's "seen some things," as my grandma would say. Been through a lot. His clothes are patched together, super-mismatched. One of his sleeves is barely hanging on to the rest of his shirt. He walks with a slight limp. Kendall gave him some water and half a loaf of bread. She didn't want to, but Troy made her. The boy said thanks and then just sat down in the middle of the driveway and ate and drank, asked for another glass of water, drank that. He asked if we had any drugs, and we said no. He then stood up, dusted off his pants, gave us a wave, and headed down the trails toward the river.

I heard Troy tell Kendall to find the shotgun.

Real Late, After Dinner
The boy's name is Charlie.

When he came back from the river, he told us it was flooded. He was so excited about it. He said that the others would also be excited. It was just what they were looking for. It was a sign. First fire, then floods.

I tried to explain to Charlie that there's a big lake to the north. It's called Possum Kingdom. Sometimes the dams are released from there, and that causes the river to run higher and faster for a little while. It's not a sign from heaven or anything. It's totally a human-caused thing.

He wouldn't listen. He said that the water would keep rising and rising, that it would flood everything. It would sweep most of us away. After that, those of us who were left would be set upon by the animals. They'd come out of the woods and the trees. That's the phrasing he used: set upon.

Like those hawks, he said, pointing up to a great big bird that was perched on the top of a dead tree. Abby had looked up and frowned. It did seem to be watching us.

According to Charlie, those of us who were left after that—after the animals had their way—would be the lucky ones. The favored ones.

So, Troy said, trying to be cool. Where are you headed next?

Charlie just looked up to the blurred-out moon, kinda smiling. We wouldn't let Charlie in the house, but he seemed fine with that. I don't think he left the property, though. I think he's still out there.

Morning, Before Breakfast
Charlie's still here.

Morning, After Breakfast
Charlie was actually sitting at the breakfast table when I came down. Off and on, he'd try to give tips to Kendall about bread

making or how to better the ratio between coffee grounds and hot water, and it was making her really, really mad. It's sometimes fun to watch Kendall get mad, but not today.

Again, Troy asked Charlie where he planned to go next, gave him the spiel about how this land belonged to his family, and Charlie responded by sitting back all comfy-cozy in his chair and saying something like "the land belongs to everyone," which I <u>know</u> Troy didn't like hearing.

Charlie said he'd been traveling with a group of people from Ennis. He'd been sent ahead to find a place for them to settle and wait out the Judgment: the floods, the animals, etc.

<u>And when I saw this house and this river,</u> he said. <u>I knew . . .</u>

I saw Kendall tense up. She was standing at the counter, but all of a sudden, she spun around, gripping her rolling pin in her hand.

<u>You can't stay here,</u> she said.

Charlie didn't reply.

<u>You can't stay here!</u> Kendall yelled.

No one talked for the rest of breakfast.

Later, Before Dinner

Charlie also has immigrant parents. Both of them are from Mexico. After breakfast, when I was sitting out back by myself, he came out and asked me what it's like to live with all these white people, and I told him about growing up around here, in a majority-white rural community, and then about going to a majority-white private school, and said that I was used to it. And that I usually felt accepted.

I could tell he wasn't buying it. Sometimes I don't even buy it myself.

He told me that his group of travelers came from all kinds of backgrounds. The eruption of Pilot Knob had shaken more than just the land—also their beliefs, their ideas about themselves as people and how they wanted to live out their last days. The way he was talking today was different from the way he was talking last night. I mean, he was still prophesying the apocalypse, but his tone was way less crazed.

That's why we came to this house, I responded. We wanted to be by ourselves.

Is that true, though? he asked. You want to be alone?

This made me think not about Troy and Abby and Kendall and Steph, but about Case, and how she's coming soon, next week. And how I don't want to be alone because I want to see her so much.

I told Charlie about her, about the fire. His eyes got real big, and he said that he would be honored to meet her when she gets here and talk to her about what it was like to escape death and essentially be reborn.

He is the kind of person Case would absolutely hate talking to.

Morning, After Breakfast
Charlie didn't sleep in the house last night, but he did join us for breakfast again. Troy said, before lunch, we should all go down to the river together, and see what this flood was all about, see if the water was still as high.

Case is halfway down the stairs when she stops. There are people in the den. They're making noise, but they're not talking. Listening more closely, Case can hear the slip and slide of clothes and mouths, the soft crunch of fabric. Troy grunts, and Abby lets out a soft sigh. Leather squeaks. There's wetness: lips on lips.

Case tiptoes the rest of the way down, across the entryway, through the empty kitchen to grab her bandanna out of her bag, and out again, into the thick-air afternoon. She's acting like a ghost. She's vanishing, which is what people at this house seem to be doing a lot of lately.

Her plan was to vanish to the river and then on to Andrea's camp. Once there, Case would shake the bugs out of the hammock, string it back up, sit, and read through Andrea's pages again, try to make sense of them.

What happened? What happened at the river? Did they even make it out there? That was the last page: a plan for a trip to a swollen river. Drea must've known something could happen there, which is why she stashed her papers in the wall in the bathroom—unless she *always* stashed her papers in the wall in the bathroom.

But Case can't get to Drea's camp. The river is, in fact, too high. Steph was right. The water has risen to the point that Case can't cross—*won't* cross—and the current of the mud-brown water is fast. She watches a tree branch enter her field of vision from the left and counts off four seconds until it passes in front of her.

It has to be the same thing Drea had described. The lake. Possum Kingdom. The lovely lake with the unfortunate name, where Case went canoeing a couple of rare times with her mom and Walter. That lake was created by a dam, and if you drive out far enough you can see that dam off one of the nearby roads. Someone must've opened it, and what Case is currently witnessing is the result.

Case lets out a quiet hum of dread. This water, moving this way, can change things. It can disturb what *was* here, rustle things up. It can wash things away, bring in new things. There are things beneath the surface that are being carried by the currents. Things in the things.

Case doesn't believe that a swollen river is a sign from a vengeful god, but she believes it's a sign of *something*—and typically not something good.

And then, for the briefest moment, Case thinks she hears a hog again, which is exactly the kind of awful thing that could be rustled up by the rising river, but when she spins around, she quickly realizes it's not a hog. It's Steph. The girl stumbles from the path, her face lit up, clearly glad to have found Case.

"Sorry if I scared you," Steph says. "I thought you might be out here. I was just wondering if you wanted to see my chickens."

On the tip of Case's tongue is: *Who is Charlie?*

Abby lied earlier about him being "someone from school." Where is this Charlie? Did he take Andrea away? But Case doesn't really want the answers to these questions from Steph. She wants them from Troy. The one who flat-out lied when he said that Drea must've gone to go see her mom, the one who failed to mention that some seriously fucked-up shit went down at this house just a few days ago.

"The chickens," Case says instead. "Right. Sure."

Steph leads the way to her henhouse, down a winding deer trail, which is basically a strip of mashed grass. Through the occasional breaks in the trees, Case catches glimpses of White Sky, an imposing image that's somehow able to push through even the densest orange murk.

"What?" Steph says, looking over her shoulder. "What's funny?"

"What's what?" Case blinks.

"What's funny?" Steph repeats, pulling her bandanna down so that her voice isn't as muffled. "You were thinking about something. You were smiling."

"Oh. I guess I was thinking about that hill over there."

"And it made you smile?" Steph asks. "Hills make you smile?"

"I guess so."

Steph grins before pushing the cloth back over her mouth and nose. "Hills make me smile, too."

The girl ducks low between a couple of oaks, then skirts around a wide cedar. Case follows. It's here that the deer path connects with a well-trodden footpath, and a minivan-sized building made of red-painted wood comes into view. Like the main house, the coop is also rough and slumped. A few chickens are hanging around, making their bubble-throated sounds and pecking lazily at the dirt.

"These flowers are new." Steph squats in the middle of the path. "They just started popping up the other day."

She reaches out to graze the small white petals with her fingertip, in a gentle gesture that reminds Case of her driver from earlier and the way he touched the photos on his dashboard.

"It's a rain lily," Case says.

Steph looks up. "You know the names of flowers?"

"Some of them."

A rust-red hen, prompted by the sound of voices, breaks apart from a cluster of other chickens and comes trotting over. Steph waits in a crouch until she can scoop up the bird. She rises, holding the hen to her chest.

"This one loves me," Steph beams. "Her name is Gertie."

Case remembers the name from Drea's pages. She looks at the bird's feet and can see that its scales are still swollen from the mites.

"She's pretty," Case says truthfully. She's always liked red animals: horses, chickens, dogs. "You have names for all of them?"

"Oh yeah. They're all so different, so it's easy to tell them apart. Aside from Gertie, though, I don't think most of them like me to hang around so much."

A curious black hen struts over, and Case kneels to meet it. She reaches her hand out, palm-side down, the way you're supposed to introduce yourself and your scent to an unfamiliar creature. In response, the hen pecks sharply at Case's first knuckle.

"Ow!" she cries out. "*Jesus.*"

Case looks at her hand and winces. The chicken has drawn blood. A cut right there at the joint will take forever to heal.

"Sorry," Steph says. "That's Sonya. She's sorta mean."

"It's fine." Case shakes out her hand and stands. She gestures in the direction of the coop. "Introduce me to the others."

There are at least a dozen hens, and Steph ticks off their names, one after the other, as she offers them a few handfuls of feed. Miss Pris is a bully, shouldering past the others to get to food. Tammie's pecking is lazy, like she can hardly be bothered to eat. Annabel walks in a slight counterclockwise arc. Hilde sleeps while the other hens swarm around her. Martha stands to the side, glaring at the others like she's plotting her revenge.

In between introductions, Steph tells Case about her plans. Getting a whole new house for the chickens would be ideal, of course, but that's impossible, so she'll settle for some new wire and boards to fill in the gaps. Troy has promised to get the materials soon.

"The price of flour has gone up so much, though," Steph adds. "So we have to save our money for that right now."

God forbid Kendall go a couple of days without baking bread.

"This is Mae," Steph says as a large white hen struts over. "Andrea named her."

Case grins. Mae was the name of Andrea's favorite chicken back in Millsap. Just like this one, Mae was big and white. Mae hated Case. And she wouldn't only peck at her, like Sonya. Whenever Case would open the gate on the chain-link fence and try to cross the yard to the front door of Andrea's house, Mae would come charging full tilt, squawking with her wings spread wide.

"Andrea told you she kept chickens, right?" Case asks. "In her backyard?"

"She did, yeah," Steph says.

Andrea never let anyone butcher her hens, but their ultimate fate might not have been much better. When Andrea left for the boarding school, she donated all of them to the agriculture program at the high school. They weren't particularly cared for there, and Case heard they eventually got depressed and started plucking out their own feathers.

"You know Andrea wrote all the time?" Case asks. "She kept journals and notebooks and things like that."

Steph nods.

"Do you know if she kept those anywhere, like, hid them in places aside from her room?"

Case is playing a hunch. Steph seems like a protector—not an unhinged quasi-housewife like her sister, but, if her demeanor around her chickens is an indicator, a genuine caretaker. She might know where her housemates would stash their precious things.

Before Steph can answer, several of her chickens start squawking, and both girls look over to the path to see Kendall approaching, wearing a bandanna around her nose and mouth and carrying a double-barreled shotgun over her shoulder.

Baking bread, holding a weapon—somehow they both make sense when it comes to Kendall.

"Did you fire off a shot earlier this morning?" Case asks.

"I did," Kendall replies. "There's a coyote around. It's been getting into the chickens." Kendall turns to Steph. "Did you decide yet?" she asks.

The younger girl doesn't answer, just sort of scrunches her face in defiance.

"They're not your pets," Kendall goes on to say. "They're food."

"They're *not* food!" Steph snaps.

"The others said they wanted one for dinner." Kendall points the barrel of the gun toward the chicken house. "That's why we got them. That's why they're here—for us to *eat*. I'm going to go out and look for coyotes again, but I'm coming back later. You have to choose one, or I'll choose myself."

Kendall continues on her way down the path, in the direction of the river. Case watches until she disappears and then pivots toward Steph, who is surveying her chickens, her eyes narrowed as she weighs her impossible decision.

"I'm sorry." It's the only thing Case can think to say. "That seems really mean, especially because Abby just went out for groceries."

"There's no fridge here," Steph says. "I mean, there *is* a fridge, but it's never worked. The one time Abby brought back a chicken from the store, it sat out all day and then Troy got sick. After that, we bought the chickens from the ranch supply. They were really little then, just barely hatched. Andrea helped me raise them."

The thing about Troy getting sick doesn't make sense. Even if there's no working fridge, they all know that every gas station and convenience store in the county sells bags of ice and Styrofoam coolers. Also, a butchered bird could sit out for a few hours, cool to room temperature, and not go bad. The whole killing-chickens-for-dinner thing seems like just another part of the strange rural-paradise fantasy these people have going on.

Again, Case weighs her words, trying to figure out the best way to get more information from Steph without causing her to shut off.

"Was there a fight or something?" Case asks. "Before Drea left?"

"There are always fights," Steph says, but she doesn't offer any more than that. "Why?"

"I'm just still trying to figure out where she is, where she could've gone."

Steph pauses, gazing at the path that Kendall took.

"There's a place in one of the downstairs rooms where Andrea hid things," she says after a beat. "I'll look there." Steph looks back to Case. "Every night, I read on the couch in the den, after everyone has gone to sleep. If I've found anything, I'll give it to you then. When no one else is around."

Case brings Steph into a bear hug so strong and surprising it nearly knocks off the girl's hat.

"That would be great, Steph," Case says. "You're the best."

FOUR

AT THIS POINT, Case is caught in a time loop. She's outside again, sitting at the picnic table. Troy is across from her, again with a pitcher of ice water and a half-full glass, again biting down softly on a toothpick. He's gazing into the trees, seemingly lost in thought. Case is sitting across from him, taking sips from her glass of water, pretending she wouldn't rather grab the pitcher and chug the whole thing.

Abby is in her lounge chair under the limbs of the oak. She's wearing her cop sunglasses. Her legs are stretched out, crossed at the ankles. Her sneakers are in the grass, probably being swarmed by ants, and her can of bug spray is within reach.

It's virtually the same scene as before, except for the sky. The haze has moved in fully, blocking out the direct sun, creating this weird filter that causes everything to be the color of a too-ripe peach. It isn't cooler, necessarily. But it's like a dome has been placed over this part of the world, and things are quieter and without wind. The shadows of the house and the trees don't move. The air doesn't move.

Case takes a breath and scans her body. This is another trick from all that therapy: slow your breathing, check in with yourself. Her head is pretty clear, but there's a slight throbbing behind her right ear, and something like a tickle in the crease of her right arm. Is this the result of the air or stress or an insect bite, or is it the start of something truly agonizing? Case doesn't know yet. She glances at the watch on Troy's wrist and counts the hours. It's just now four. She took a pill before nine. She shouldn't really need another one yet, but her pain doesn't come like clockwork.

When she'd made her way back to the house, Case had tried to keep quiet, assuming Troy and Abby were either still going at it or napping half-naked in each other's arms.

But they weren't. They were already out here. Sitting. Sitting silently in their respective places.

There's no reason to sit out here. Unless you somehow think you are better than this weather. Unless you somehow think the ash in the sky amplifies your radiance as opposed to clogging up your organs.

The hawks are also here again, stuck in the same time loop, perched on opposite sides of the roof. They're not facing each other, but Case can tell that each is very much aware of the other. They're assessing each other out of the corner of their eyes. One of them ruffles its pebble-colored feathers just slightly, and then the other does the same. They're playing macho head games.

Again, there's a wasp, doing what wasps do. It's hovering not above the table this time, but near a window off to the side of the house, tap-tapping against the glass pane as if it wants inside. It flies away, up to its nest, only to return a few moments later to resume its tapping. It's mesmerizing: the hovering, the insistence. Case is spellbound. The wasp floats over, hovers by Troy's ear, then zips back to the nest. He doesn't even notice.

Something that's different: Troy's hands. Case notices when he brings his glass of water up to take a sip. There are fresh scrapes on his knuckles, and a few on his wrist, near where he's cuffed his shirt. There's no blood seeping out, but the small wounds are bright pink. There's no shine of recently applied ointment. The flakes of grated flesh haven't yet dried out completely, and Case wonders how this happened, and why Abby hasn't tended to him, the way she did for her.

Case shifts in her seat. Andrea's pages are still in her pocket, making her right hip pop up a little higher than her left, making her feel tilted like the old house just behind her. Of course, what she'd rather be doing is reading those pages again. If she can't have her friend in the flesh, then she wants her friend on paper, no matter how unsettling her stories are.

Then suddenly: the crack of a shotgun.

It's so close that Abby shrieks and Case jumps in her seat, which causes her glass to tilt and precious ice water to splash across her wrist. The hawks on the roof fly away, so quickly and so violently Case can hear their talons rip the shingles.

"That was, like, right here," Case says.

"No kidding," Abby replies. "Jesus H."

"I saw Kendall in the woods a while ago," Case says. "She says she was after a coyote."

"She's ruthless," Abby says. Case can't tell if it's a compliment or a criticism.

Troy, during all this, has hardly blinked. His toothpick is stuck to his bottom lip and dangling. Again, the wasp soars past Troy's left ear, then dips so close as to nearly land on his shoulder. *Again*, Troy doesn't notice, and Case finds she doesn't have the energy to lean over and shoo the insect away.

After gulping down the rest of her water, Case pulls a piece of ice into her mouth and works on destroying it with her molars. That comparatively tiny sound—ice crunching between teeth, as opposed to the echoing crack of a shotgun—finally rattles Troy out of his daze. He shakes his head. The wasp flies away.

Case shifts again, which reminds her of the paper in her pocket, which reminds her of the bundle of letters in her bag.

"Do you consider yourself a good listener?" she asks Troy, leaning across the table.

"What?" Troy swivels his toothpick around before clamping it between his teeth.

"Do you consider yourself a good listener?" Case repeats.

Troy shrugs. "I guess it would depend on who's talking, and what's being said." He reaches for the pitcher of water and refills Case's glass before topping off his own. "Why?"

Case drinks, then waits a moment, thinking Abby might react—if not chime in with an opinion, then at least grunt or chuckle. She does nothing, though.

"No reason," Case replies. "I've just always thought that was a nice quality for a person to have: the ability to listen."

"Are you a good listener?" Troy shoots back.

Case grins. It's a wiry thing on her lips, thin and bent. "I listen to *things* more than I listen to people. Like noises, or sounds. The wind, or a dog barking. The sizzle of meat in a pan. Things like that."

"That's weird," Abby says from across the yard. "That's a weird thing to say."

"Abby's a good listener," Troy says.

"Shut up," Abby mutters.

"Good at eavesdropping anyway," he adds.

Just then, Case notices a strange shadow bouncing in the trees, off to the side of the house. She spins around to get a better look.

"Oh shit," she hears Abby say. "Holy *shit*."

Part of the shadow is cast by Kendall, who is trudging across the far side of the yard. The rest of the shadow is cast by the two things Kendall is carrying: her shotgun and a small sand-colored coyote. She has its two back legs in one hand, slung over her shoulder. The rest of the body trails behind in the dirt.

"Argh!" Abby exclaims. "What on *earth*?"

Kendall doesn't break stride and barely glances in their direction.

"Pleased with yourself?" Case calls out.

The girl keeps on walking. Eventually, she shifts her hands to get a better grip on the coyote. Its forepaws and the side of its head drag across the rough ground. Case catches a glimpse of its pink tongue hanging out between its whitest-white teeth, and she has to look away.

"So gross," Abby says.

"It's little," Case offers. "Just a pup."

"It could've killed the chickens," Troy says.

The two hawks, once they realize they aren't the ones being hunted, fly back to the roof. After they land, they keep their wings spread wide.

"Where is Kendall going with that?" Abby asks. She's watching the birds as she talks, and sneering at them.

"To the fence, probably," Case says. "At the end of the driveway."

"Why?"

"To tie it up." Case eyes the hawks above, which, like before, during lunchtime, are taking confrontational little hops toward each other. "People string up coyotes by their legs and hang them on their fences. Their corpses are supposed to deter other coyotes from coming around."

"Ew," Abby mumbles.

"Does it work?" Troy asks. He leans across the table, suddenly all interested.

"I'm not sure," Case says. "I don't think so. I've seen fences with three or four coyotes tied to them, so obviously it didn't work in those cases. I don't actually think coyotes fear death. More likely, they would see a body strung up there and take it as a challenge."

Above, the hawks lift off in near unison, then jab tentatively at each other with their talons.

Abby makes the slightest motion, like she's reaching for her shoes. "I think that maybe we should go in—"

With a loud beat of their wings, the hawks rise into the air again and collide into a vicious knot. Tan and black feathers scatter as the birds spin, clawing at each other. Then they plummet, still tangled, toward the picnic table.

Abby cries out, and the toothpick in Troy's mouth snaps in half. All three of them—Case, Abby, Troy—are instantly on the move. Abby runs toward Troy, following him into the house, but Case is too far away, separated from the house by the picnic table. She's forced to retreat, one unsteady step at a time, toward the trees.

The hawks keep falling—screeching—until they crash together onto the table. The pitcher of water shatters, and the two glasses spin, then tumble to the dirt. There are smears of red on the bench where Case was just sitting. The birds have sliced each other open and drawn blood.

"Oh my god," Case breathes.

Even though one or both are injured, instead of flying away, or even fighting over the food scraps that might've been left under the table from lunch, the birds take flight, break away from each other, and crash together again. Then they soar straight through the open doors and into the house.

More glass breaks. Furniture squeals across the floor. A lamp or a vase or some other delicate thing slides from a surface and explodes on the ground. These are the sounds that Case can hear from outside, as well as something (a hawk? a shoulder? a fist?) bumping against a door or a wall, then bumping into it again and again.

Above all that, the worst sound—the one that makes Case want to cover her ears, crouch down, and burrow herself into the dirt—is the constant, urgent flapping of bird wings in a space where birds shouldn't be flapping their wings. She remembers, once, a long time ago, the panicked fluttering of a bird caught in the crawl space under her house, and the way its little body thumped against the floorboards. Over the course of a day, that fluttering and thumping got less panicked, less frequent, and then stopped altogether.

From inside this house, Abby is shrieking. Troy is shouting at her to *move*, to *get back*.

Case starts to hear something else, something different—the scrape of metal against stone. That slow scrape is what finally draws her to the house. She scoots around the picnic table, slowly advancing toward the open door. She stops momentarily when glass explodes again, but then carries on. The flapping continues, but there's also a groan, a whoosh, and a series of squeaks. Something is swinging. Case imagines the birds have collided with a light fixture—a chandelier or a fan. Bracing one hand against the doorframe, Case peers in, half expecting to see wings tangled up near the ceiling in chains and tiny crystals.

Yes, a chandelier *is* swinging, but the birds aren't knotted up in it. Case doesn't actually see them at first. She scans the room, which is an in-progress disaster—toppled furniture, torn curtains, scattered books and book pages. The twelve-point stag is still perched on the wall above the fireplace, but it's now been kicked to the side about thirty degrees and staring at her slantways.

Abby tries to make a mad dash across the room, but the hawks cut her off, swooping from one of the bookshelves, careening in her direction. Luckily, they miss her, going wide and slamming as a single unit into a side table. A lamp teeters. Abby stoops to catch it before it falls, and then clutches it to her chest like it's the most precious thing in the world.

The low scraping sound Case heard was from Troy retrieving an iron poker from beside the fireplace. He's holding it in his right hand, down by his side, spinning the handle in his palm. He's watching the birds and breathing hard. There's a wicked, semi-murderous gleam in his eye.

"Do it!" shouts Abby.

Troy takes the poker in both hands and hoists it over his shoulder like a baseball bat. The aim is tricky here. The iron tool is so heavy that if Troy misses the birds, he won't be able to self-correct his swing and might cause even more damage, crashing into the wall or a table or Abby.

Troy takes a step forward and grimaces. He's in ready position, about to take his shot, but then the birds fly too close and he loses his nerve.

Abby shouts again: "Troy, *now!*"

Case is still watching things unfold from her place just outside the door—the throb behind her ear getting stronger, more insistent, blowing up like a balloon—but soon something else catches her eye. Straight through the wreck of the room, on the table in the entryway close to the front door: Abby's keys and that little purple puff.

Case could escape this place, find cell reception, find the county sheriff, and show them what Drea wrote. But her attention is pulled back to the room when Troy finally swings, swiping sideways. He misses the birds by a good two feet, and momentum carries him around. He spins like a dancer, a full one-eighty turn, and the tip of the poker lodges itself into the back of a couch. Troy grunts as he struggles to wrench it out.

"Kendall!" yells Troy—loud, hoping his voice will carry outside the house, through the trees, down the lane. "Shotgun!"

"No shotgun!" cries Abby.

Abby's right. For obvious reasons, it would be very bad to fire a shotgun at a moving target in the middle of a house.

The birds, meanwhile, are still focused on their own fight, though it's clear they're tiring out. Their battle was vicious but brief. Their wings are now beating with a little less force. They make a wide circle around the ceiling, and then land, separately, and start to nudge at their wounds with their beaks. One of them is gripping the edge of a coffee table, scraping gouges in the polished wood. The other is on the floor, on the faded carpet. A hunk of white fluff from the couch cushions or a throw pillow is caught in its talons.

This is Troy's chance. He lunges forward, bringing up the poker to swing again, but Case rushes in. She hurdles over a toppled chair and stops his arm with the grip of both her hands.

"Stop!" she demands. "They'll fly out on their own."

Troy turns to Case. He's still got a mad look in his eyes, and his breathing has gone erratic.

"They *will*," Case says. She doesn't know how she knows this. She just does. "Just let them."

Troy is hardly swayed. His white shirt is soaked through with sweat, the fabric now stuck to his chest. He's glaring at the birds and still white-knuckling the handle of the poker.

Case is sure he is going to kill them, or at least try, but then from the outside, there's an unexpected break in the still afternoon air—so sudden everyone looks to the door to see the shredded drapes billow and pop and, beyond that, the leaves in the trees spinning on their branches.

Out in the western sky, there's a strong line of clouds pushing through the haze, dark, like silicate minerals. Storms might be coming.

The hawks must see this as a sign. They take off, one after the other, out of the house and into the woods. Case has been holding on to Troy's arm all this time, trying to steady him, but now she drops it and steps back.

"What was that?" Abby asks, turning to Case—as if Case would know the answer. "I mean . . ."

"I don't know," Case says. "I've never seen anything like that before."

Abby walks over to a side table, her legs unsteady. Gently, she sets down the lamp she's been cradling and works to straighten the shade. She looks around, leans over to grab one of the throw pillows that isn't completely destroyed, and tosses it across the room to Troy, who snatches it out of the air with one hand. His eyes are still wild, but he throws down his poker, which lands with a clatter on the stones near the fireplace.

Kendall appears, too late. She's flushed from running. Her shotgun hangs by her side. When she sees what's happened, she lets out a small moan and collapses sideways into the doorframe.

"We don't need you anymore," Troy says.

Kendall deflates further, shrinking against the door. Case imagines it's a terrible thing for Kendall to hear: that she's not necessary.

"What happened?" the girl asks.

"We had a problem with some birds," Abby replies—as if that explains anything.

Kendall doesn't respond. She just gapes at Abby, clearly confused.

Abby stoops again, this time to pick up a book that was knocked loose from the shelves. When she straightens up, she turns, facing Kendall directly.

"We had a *problem*," Abby repeats slowly, "with some *birds*."

Case tries, but she's unable to hold back her laughter. It starts off as a series of snorts, but then explodes into full-blown cackles. A moment later, Abby joins in. Before long, Case can barely breathe. She has to sit on the couch to catch her breath, but her cackles only get louder when she glances to the cushions and to the clouds of white fluff that are pushing out through a giant rip in green velvet.

"A problem," Case gasps, "with some birds."

Abby is laughing so hard she's hiccuping. She moves behind Case, bracing herself against the back of the couch.

Case tries covering her mouth, which somehow makes everything worse. Her eyes are watering to the point that she can hardly see.

"I'm sorry," Case says with a snort. "I'm so sorry."

"What a bitch," Kendall mutters, and Abby laughs so hard her screeches rival those of the hawks.

Really, though. What kind of hard-hearted person laughs at the misfortune of others? Hoots in the aftermath of a mini-disaster? Could it possibly be the same type of person who is plotting to steal a car?

It's that puff—that ridiculous purple puff on the entry hall table. It's taunting Case. It's been taunting her for hours. Even as she's doubled over laughing on the couch, she's homed in mentally on its position: a few feet behind her, through an open doorway. From that table, it's just a few feet to the front door. From the front door, it's just a few short strides to the car.

Case is fast, and she can be quiet. She could be gone before anyone notices. The only thing giving her pause is the possibility she'll receive more of Drea's writing from Steph later. But this gift of escape is something she can't ignore.

Case is itchy. Case is giddy. There's a new giddiness layered on top of the recent bird-induced giddiness. She thinks, *This is it*. The outside world will help her now. She'll go back to Timmy's. She'll find a landline. She'll call troopers with her remaining quarter and tell them about her missing friend and some weirdo named Charlie and the papers her friend left hidden in the house. Who knows? Maybe there's more writing in other walls. The cops will come out here, search the house to figure out what happened, and, hopefully, break the whole place apart in the process. Case is even more giddy as she imagines Kendall hemming and hawing about overripe raspberries, and how she has bread in the oven that's about to burn, and how they—the cops, the *intruders*—are ruining everything.

Case has to time this just right. Her wide-mouthed cackles soon soften to giggles, and she's able to wipe her bleary eyes clear. Around her, the housemates have gone silent in their work. Abby, a dopey grin plastered to her face, is still picking up books one by one, holding them out like dirty socks when they flap open on their broken spines. Kendall surveys the damage for a long while, then leaves to grab a broom from the kitchen, to sweep up feathers and broken glass, she says. Troy is righting some of the furniture—aligning wooden feet with the joints of the floorboards—but mostly looking around with a frown. Occasionally, he lifts his sour gaze to the open back door, to where the hawks have disappeared. His eyes narrow, as if he's hatching some revenge plot. Or maybe he's scared. Maybe he thinks Charlie's prophecy is coming true. First fire, then floods, then being *set upon* by the animals.

Case is looking to the open back door as well, not plotting her revenge, necessarily, but plotting her next move. But then, in flies a wasp. Of course, it's impossible to tell if it's the same wasp from earlier, because all wasps look essentially the same, but Case would like to think it's the same one. It finally got what it wanted. It doesn't have to tap on the glass anymore. It's inside now, doing a big lap around the room, over everyone's heads, until it lands on the coffee table, just in front of where Case is sitting. Specifically, it lands on the cover of a fashion magazine. Even more specifically, it lands on the sleeve of a bright pink dress that the cover model is wearing. That wasp thinks the dress is a flower. It keeps dipping its little wasp head down toward the glossy paper. First, the wasp wanted to tap its way through a glass door. Now, it wants to suck nectar from paper. It seems to love impossible tasks. It's a glutton for punishment—an annoying, persistent thing.

Still loopy from laughing, Case grins. She can also be an annoying, persistent thing.

No one else notices the wasp. They're all too busy trying to put things in order. It's a good time to make a break for it. While Abby is preoccupied, carrying a teetering stack of hardcovers across the room, and Troy's back is turned, Case rises from the couch and slips into the entryway. She soundlessly swipes the puff and the attached keys from the table, pushes through the front door, and is outside once again.

Abby's car is very old, so Case has to unlock it manually. Even though she's fairly certain she made no noise during her escape, she still nervously fumbles with the keys, casting glances over her shoulder to the house, until the lock gives. After falling into the seat behind the wheel, Case starts the engine and shifts the car into drive.

At this point, there's no more stealth. Case guns it, and, as gravel and dust flies from out behind the tires, she makes a hard three-point turn to get oriented in the right direction.

Case's fantasy of escape is short-lived, though. When she steers the car around the bend in the driveway, she's immediately forced to slam on the brakes. There's debris blocking the narrow lane, a mess of tangled branches and some hollow logs. None of this was here before.

She can see drag marks along the ground, dark and new, leading from the woods. The mess in front of her isn't from a tree that's fallen or been blown over by weak wind. It's been pulled into the lane intentionally, to prevent this car from getting out—or to prevent any other car from coming in.

A memory slides into place: Troy's hands from earlier, those fresh-looking scrapes along his knuckles.

He came out here. *He* did this.

Case shifts the car into park, jumps out, shoves the keys into her front pocket so that the puff dangles out by her hip, and starts tossing the least heavy branches out of the path. None of this is impossible to move; it's just going to take time. Case ignores the mesquite barbs that jab into her palm, as well as the sweat that's beginning to pool at her lower back. She makes a point not to look down the lane, toward that rickety monster of a house. All she focuses on is the act of grabbing branches, then throwing them. Grabbing, then throwing.

There is still hope and time. She will get reception. She will call the cops. The cops will come.

At first, Case pretends she doesn't hear the sound of someone stalking in her direction—the slow, deliberate crunch of gravel underfoot—but after she hauls away another bunch of branches, she looks up and sees Troy. The fireplace poker is down by his side, its iron tip angled toward the ground.

"You thought I couldn't move some branches myself?" Case shouts.

Troy doesn't reply. Case notices the wrinkles in his white shirt and the sheen of sweat on his neck. He takes a hard swallow, then advances—not toward Case, but toward the back end of the car. In one smooth motion, he lifts up the poker, then slams it down. This time, his aim is true. The curled tip lodges deep into the rubber of the tire, and Troy leaves it there, releasing the handle and stepping back.

The tire hisses as it flattens. The sound is so loud and eerie that Case can't help but cringe. She watches the car sag and tilt. It sinks slowly, like the sun setting in summer.

Abby and Kendall come running around the bend, but they both stop when they see the car and what Troy has done. An expression warps Abby's face—betrayal, Case thinks—and a quick shine of tears forms in her eyes.

"What did you do?" Abby asks in a whisper. Then louder: "What the *fuck* did you do, Troy?"

"You might have taken her," Troy says. "Driven her to the city."

"I . . ." Abby trails off. She puts one hand to her ear to muffle the sound of the still-hissing tire. "I wouldn't have done that."

"You *might* have," Kendall chimes in. "Out of all of us, you're the most sympathetic."

"Sympa—" Abby sputters. "I need the car! *We* need the car!"

"There are other cars," Troy says. "I can get us another car."

Abby spins around in a half circle, lifts her gaze to the treetops, and lets out a scream.

"In the meantime, there's a spare tire in the cellar," Troy adds. "It's flat, but if we end up needing it, I can figure out a way to get some air in it." He pauses. "Give me those."

Troy holds out his hand toward Case, his palm facing up. He waits a second, then does that impatient *Come on, come on* gesture, twitching his fingers inward toward his wrist. He's asking Case to give him the keys like she's a child who's been caught sneaking a cookie.

"Give it," he urges.

Case lets out a huff of disbelief. This whole time, she's been clutching a tree branch, which she now drops to the ground. She then reaches into her pocket to draw the keys out by their puff and walks toward Troy.

When Case gets close enough, she hefts the keys once, into her hand, and then throws them. She's aiming for Troy's throat, specifically the tender hollow between his collarbones, but the keys instead collide with his bottom lip. Troy bucks back in shock. He tries to catch the keys as they bounce off his chin, but they fall to the ground.

Case bends down swiftly, scoops up the keys, and then pitches them sideways, deep into the trees. They create a rustle when they land, hopefully in the middle of a bramble patch.

"There you go," she says.

Abby looks into the trees as if they were an ocean and her keys had been lost to some deep, impenetrable depth.

"By the way," Case says, taking a breath, "the cops are coming. In case Abby didn't tell you, when we went to town earlier, I gave the people who worked at the store the address of this house. I told them I was in danger, and to call the troopers."

"No, you didn't," Kendall says, but there's a hitch in her voice that gives her uncertainty away. She looks past Case, down the lane that leads to the highway. "They would be here by now."

"Would they?" Case counters.

"Abby," Troy says. His hand is covering his mouth, but Case can see a smudge of watery blood there. "Is that true?"

Kendall spins toward Abby, who is still sadly gazing into the trees.

"Abby, why didn't you say anything?" Kendall demands. "You *are* the sympathetic one."

"Christ, calm down," Abby says. "That's just what Case told me. For all we know, she could be lying."

"I also told them about Charlie," Case says, playing her ace.

Everyone freezes.

"I know all about him," Case goes on to say. "I know about Charlie, and the river, and—"

"No, you don't," Kendall counters, cutting Case off. "Don't lie."

"I do know. Drea told me in a letter. I know about the birds, how Charlie said they'd attack. And that's what they just did. It's the start of something."

"There's *no way* that's possible." Kendall then looks to Troy, helplessly. "What is she talking about? Why is this happening? Why is everything falling apart?"

"I don't know," Troy says. Then he swiftly switches gears. "Nothing is falling apart. Everything is fine."

"*Nothing is fine,*" Kendall bellows.

"Everything fell apart a long time ago," Abby adds. "Like, back when the ground exploded and fire started spewing into the sky."

"Look, I'm sorry," Case says, though she's not sorry at all. She starts slowly backing down the driveway, keeping the trio in her sights. "But your time out here is up."

Kendall moves so fast—rushing forward, pushing past Troy. She tugs the fireplace poker from the flat tire of Abby's car. Case sees a face contorted into fury, straight teeth bared, the tip of a braid, a dark blur, and then nothing but white dust.

There's a sound inside Case's head, like the satisfying *plink* of a stone breaking the surface of still water. It ripples.

PART TWO:

NIGHT

CASE IS INSIDE—inside a building or just inside her own head, she's not sure. It's dark, but there's a mustard-yellow light, a faraway dot, over to the side. She tries to reach it, tries moving, but her body refuses. She wants to call out to the light, but her tongue is too big and too dry to make a sound. Again, she tries to move. It's a massive effort. She tells her brain to tell her nerves to tell her arms to reach or her legs to run, but nothing happens.

That dot of light—it doesn't move, doesn't hover or dim. It doesn't care about Case.

Time has passed. Right? Case is awake. Maybe? She's awake but still stuck. The light is still there. It seems brighter now, and the shape is different: oblong, like the dot has been stretched, pulled like taffy. This time, Case doesn't try to move her legs, but instead she tries to turn her head, which leads to a bolt of terrible, clear pain and a lot more light. Light everywhere, bright white and then red. The pain and the light cause her whole body to jerk. That movement produces a sound, a nonhuman squeak from somewhere beneath her. This is the moment Case realizes she's trapped—like, *really* trapped.

Her head, though—what a mess. The pain there is growing, actually *unfurling*, like the thick, individual petals of a flower, but Case tries again to move. There's a twitch behind her right eye. When she swallows and releases, it feels like she's pulling her lungs into her throat and then shoving them back out. Case can move her head side to side, up and down, but when she does that, even slightly, she's stabbed through the temple. Her legs are too heavy, so she tries an arm, which budges slightly but is caught on something.

She takes a breath in through her nose—that, at least, feels normal. There's a smell: damp air, mold, the clean rot of compost. It's not entirely unpleasant. She takes a few more full inhales and exhales through her nose—gets her breath to a normal rhythm—and then, finally, screws up the courage to open her eyes again.

She's in a room. The light is from a small window, above her head, where the ceiling meets the wall. The color of the light isn't yellow anymore. It's now the purest, freshest watermelon pink, and the beam is coming in hard, at an angle, crossing the length of the room, a row of shelves, a closed door, a dirt floor, and the dusty tips of Case's boots.

Sunset. The sun is setting. The window must face west, because that's the only way the light could make these kinds of patterns.

A dirt floor and a perched-high window. What else? On either side of the room, there are shelves packed with . . .

Case squints. Jars. Aluminum cans. Paint cans. Coffee cans. Plastic storage baskets. Wound-up lengths of rope and garden hoses. Nozzles for those garden hoses. The split wooden handles of old farm tools. On the floor, leaning against one of the shelves, is a spare tire, flat.

A spare tire, flat.

Why is that familiar?

Case sucks in a breath. The quick action hurts her nostrils and triggers another quick, sharp pain in her head, but it also brings a shock of clarity. She's in a cellar, *the* cellar. There's a spare tire in the cellar, that one guy had said—that one guy named *Troy*.

Noises come from above Case's head. There's a thump, then a bang, then another bang. Case gasps. She knows those noises, too: the sounds of a violent baker.

The angle of the light is changing, and Case knows that darkness will come soon. Again, she tries to move but can't—not quite. She can kick one leg, the right one, but it only scrapes the dust in a semicircle. Her left leg is stuck. When Case angles her head to look down, she can see her left lower leg tied to the leg of a chair. She then realizes that her upper body is also mostly stuck because someone tied her torso to the chair, as well.

Case's heart beats faster, wildly. Historically, bad things have happened to her when she's been stuck inside dark buildings at night. Since it hurts so much to move her head, Case twists her entire upper body side to side to try and wring herself free. She then changes tactics and rocks back and forth, slamming her shoulders against the chair. The rope rasps through the fabric of her shirt and against her arms, but Case has faith in her scarred and sturdy skin.

Soon, there's a pop. One of the joints in the chair has come loose, just behind her right hip. When she wiggles her butt, the entire chair wiggles with her. Case is certain she can break the chair, but she'll have to break it against something. The best and closest option is the floor.

Instead of twisting or rocking, Case now sways. She pushes off her untethered right foot—once, then twice. The chair starts to tilt. Case *also* starts to tilt, and her whole body tenses as she braces for impact.

Case blacked out again, which she probably should have expected. When she comes to, the pain in her head is a full-blown riot. She can barely open her eyes. So she opens one, the left one, only a little. There's a shaft of light on the ground, still that fresh pink color, and she knows she couldn't have been out for too long, because the sun is still in the process of setting.

She's sideways. Her left shoulder is against the ground and throbbing from the impact. Her left wrist, though— she can wriggle it free, at least fre*er* than before. When she shimmies, things loosen even more. Just as she'd hoped, the joints of the chair busted apart when she hit the floor.

Case scoots and then bucks, lifts herself the best she can and then slams herself into the floor again. The screws that hold the remaining pieces of the chair together squeal with the strain.

She counts to ten, closes her eyes, and breathes. Her headache has now taken a shape, the way that puffy clouds do on a bright day. The shape is like a pine cone, sort of oval but with a bunch of hard, blunted spikes. Case takes another breath to try and smooth out those spikes, and it works some. She needs to stop thinking about her head and think about the rest of her body.

The ropes around her right hand are looser than the ones around the left. She sucks in a sharp breath and tries to pull her right arm straight up, like she's trying to start a lawn mower, then she does it again, straining the rope. On the third attempt, her arm flies high, part of the chair still attached to it by a length of rope.

She's free. Sort of. It's a start.

After unwinding the rope, Case gently reaches her fingers to her throbbing head. There's a knot there, above her left temple, and a painful, squishy place, but no blood. She doesn't come across anything matted or sticky as she pats along her hairline. Case flinches, remembering how the fireplace poker flew toward her head. But what she'll remember most of all—forever, probably—is the sound the poker made as it cut through the warm air. A slight *snick*, like the click of a bird's beak.

Case taps her fingers around again, still expecting to find a gaping hole in her skull. How the tip of that poker didn't sink into her brain the way it sank into the tire of Abby's car, Case has no idea.

Case shakes off the rest of the rope, stands, then immediately stumbles. Her left foot is completely asleep from being immobile for who knows how long. She lunges forward to lean against the side of one of the metal shelves, pats her back pocket to make sure Andrea's pages are still there, and thinks.

The glow of the sunset is gentle on Case's still-wobbly vision. She knows she'll have to battle her way out of this house, then off this land. But she has nothing. No tools, no weapons. Her phone is, again, gone. She needs . . . things. And it just so happens that this cellar is full of things.

Once her foot is stable enough to stand on, Case moves. She grabs a length of the rope, threads it through a belt loop, and then winds the rest into a loose coil that hangs by her hip like a lasso.

She searches through a rusted coffee can on one of the shelves, finds a folding knife and a plastic cigarette lighter, and slides both into her pockets. On another shelf, there's a red shop rag, splotched with what looks like motor oil, and next to that is a metal can of linseed oil, which Case knows is flammable under the right conditions. She ties the red rag to the handle of the linseed oil and, as quietly as she can, sets it down by the door.

There are tools hanging everywhere—hammers and wrenches and a hacksaw—but Case needs something more portable. Her gaze lands on a flathead screwdriver, which she puts into a pocket alongside the knife.

She grabs the can of linseed oil and starts creeping up the stairs.

It appears as if the stairs go nowhere, like they dead-end into the ceiling. They don't, though. What appears to be a ceiling is actually a floor—the main floor of the house. Case can see muted streams of light coming in through the edges. She stops and waits, listening for footsteps or chatter, or Kendall's angry kitchen thumps and bumps. There's nothing.

Placing her palm on the wooden slats above her head, Case braces her weight and pushes.

Case is a mouse, her face emerging from a crack in the floor, her nostrils flaring. It's too dark to see anything except a strip of pale light coming from underneath yet *another* door, but all that light does is illuminate the specks of dust against the rough grain of the wood floor. She can smell that dust—dust smells clean, like fresh parsley, but also dirty, like old sheets. Also, though, there's the thick and tangy scent of used cooking oil. Dinner must be over.

Case slides the can of linseed oil into place, using it to prop the cellar door, and now she's able to use both her hands to push herself through the opening and out into the dark room. It's a pantry, Case realizes, once she's fully inside. White bags of flour stand out on the shelves, puffed up like the chests of proud children and tidily arranged with their labels facing out. There's a row of stacked pots, and on the shelf above those, a collection of glass jars.

Case steps forward, and can see, in neat print, words written on white labels—PLUM, MIXED FRUIT, BLUEBERRY— along with dates, as far back as four months ago and as recent as last week. Case makes a half turn, and there on another shelf are dishes, matching white: plates, saucers, soup bowls, teacups, a gravy boat, a sugar bowl, and a serving platter. There are enough settings for a large party—as if that would ever happen here—and every dish looks perfect, not chipped or streaked with fine cracks.

These are Kendall's things. Neat, ready, waiting. Case is suddenly queasy, feeling like she's literally emerged from the floor into another girl's body.

The one door in this room must lead straight to the kitchen. There's a door in the kitchen that leads directly outside. *Outside* this terrible house. There are two doors between Case and her escape.

Case has to get out, she knows, but she has choices. She can save herself, which would mean plowing through this door, through the kitchen, out of the house, up the lane, to the highway, into the looming dark in the unforgiving country, without a flashlight and nothing but a screwdriver, a plastic lighter, a pocketknife, a can of linseed oil, and a piece of rope.

But it's not like anyone could follow her, because Troy ruined the car.

Her other choice: She could burn the house down.

She could soak the rag in the linseed oil, set that rag on top of the stove, and let the pilot light catch it and do its work. That doesn't seem like too bad of an idea. She survived one burning house. She could survive another.

Right?

Case doesn't know what to do. She's thinking and trying to listen for noises. And doing these things with a massive pine-cone-shaped headache is hard.

Finally, once Case is again certain she hears no signs of life, she pushes the pantry door open. The smell of used cooking oil is stronger now. The kitchen is darkening, and there's a light coming from above the counter, right next to the stove. It's a night-light, in the shape of a star.

Oh, Kendall, Case thinks, *how thoughtful of you to leave a night-light on so that Troy won't stumble when he comes down in the dark for a glass of water.*

And Case can see her phone miraculously sitting right there on the counter, like a gift, as if perfectly, purposely placed in her line of sight.

If this *is* a gift, Case will take it, but her relief in finding her phone is fleeting.

Right now, she's vulnerable, out in the open. If she hears someone approach, she probably won't have time to duck back into the pantry and hide. There's a butcher knife within reach, though, just in case, stuck onto the wall by a thick strip of a magnet. She imagines that Kendall used it earlier, before dinner, to whack the head off one of Steph's chickens.

God, Case thinks, *I hate this house.*

SEVEN THIRTY-EIGHT

WHEN CASE PICKS UP HER PHONE, the screen flashes to life and shows the time: 7:38. She's lost almost three hours. On her home screen, there's another message from Bryan, sent about an hour ago: *Still ok?*

This time, Case rushes a response: *Need help now. Pls come.* She hits SEND and then punches out a couple of other messages: one to Andrea again, another to her mom. The chances of either of them responding are next to nonexistent, but Case tries anyway.

Case hears a creak—a foot on a stair maybe. She twists her head in the direction of the sound, and that sudden movement causes an immediate and magnificent pain, radiating from her neck through her throat and into the damaged tissue of her shoulder. She buckles, goes blind for a moment, and gropes at the counter to stay upright.

Pills. They're here, across this room, in her bag on the floor.

Case treads as lightly as she can, following the counter, hand over hand, until the toe of her boot grazes the dark mass of her duffel bag. She kneels, opens the bag, and starts pushing aside her clothes and her letters—the letters she was going to give Andrea, the ones that are untied from their bundle, loose now that Troy and Kendall have sifted through and read them. Panic flares. She can't find the pill bottle. But then she does—wedged back behind a fold in the fabric.

Her fingers wrap around the familiar smoothness of the plastic, but almost immediately her panic flares brighter. Something's wrong. The bottle is too light. She shakes it, hoping desperately for the comforting rattle of pills against plastic, but there's nothing. The bottle is empty.

"Mother*fuck*," Case gasps.

This can't be right. Case had five pills left. She knows this because she *always* knows how many pills she has left.

Her brain stops working. The rest of her body stops working and then kicks into overdrive. She's shaking—her hands are, of course, but also her shoulders, and then even what feels like each of her individual ribs. The pain isn't only in her head, neck, and shoulders now, but also way down deep into her scarred right arm and needling into her spine.

Case turns on her phone's flashlight. She's searching the depths of her bag, looking for anything tiny, white, and circular. She scoots across the room to the metal trash can, thinking that if one of the roommates threw her pills away, they might be in there, sitting on the top of garbage.

When Case opens the lid, she sees the remains of dinner: small bones, gray-colored, with bits of meat still clinging in places. The flies have already found the carcass. Poor

Steph. Case hopes it wasn't Gertie who had to be sacrificed for this meal.

One of the flies soars up, straight at Case's nostrils, which causes her to jerk back. The metal lid she's holding hits the metal can. The resulting sound isn't loud, but it's clear—a resonant *ping*, like the lingering note of a tuning fork.

Someone heard that. Case *knows* someone heard that.

She nearly lets out a curse but, instead, scrunches up her face. Her phone is still in her hand. She turns off the flashlight, shoves it into her front pocket, and then dashes across the room to pick up her duffel. There's no way she's leaving Drea's letters in this house. As she pushes open the door that will lead her outside, Case half expects to come face-to-face with the housemates, all lined up and ready to hit her over the head again. But when she steps outside, there's nothing.

It's not totally dark yet, but dusk after an afternoon of orange haze is supremely gloomy. Sunsets aren't pretty anymore. They haven't been for months. There are no multi-colored stripes in the clouds. Everything just glows dully.

There's also a damp chill in the air, and an unnerving quiet.

Case's eyes will eventually adjust, but she can't stand here and wait for that to happen. Holding her duffel and armed with her stash from the cellar, she skirts the front of the house and sets off in a jog in the most hopeful of hopeless directions: down the lane and to the road.

SEVEN FORTY-THREE

THE QUICKEST AND CLEVEREST CREATURES OF THE NIGHT, like cats and coyotes and possums, are deathly quiet, detectable only by the shine of their eyes. But there are also armadillos, which are loud and sound like grown men stomping through the woods. Armadillos are shaped like little oil drums with feet. They are harmless, and not particularly brave. One night, a few months ago, when Case was taking a bath and listening in on her aunt watching *Jeopardy!* in the other room, she learned that the Germans, when they first settled in Texas, referred to armadillos as *Panzerschwein*, which translates to something like "tank pigs," which seemed about right.

Case is thinking about armadillos because she doesn't want to think about hogs, which she's sure are everywhere now, watching her from all directions. As she trots up the lane and away from the house, she swears she hears stubby legs scurrying across the dirt, or puckered snouts snorting, or brittle hooves shoving aside leaves and branches. Distracted by these sounds, Case loses her footing and trips. Both her knees hit the ground as she falls, and the screwdriver flies out of her pocket and rolls roughly across the gravel.

Case scrambles. She scoops up the duffel that fell from her arms and then rakes her fingers through the dirt for the narrow tool. When she can't find it, she quickly stands. She toes the ground for a few moments and then stops.

The most vicious tool she has left is the pocketknife, and while Case may be able to fight a *person* with a pocketknife, she sure as hell can't fight a fucking *hog* with one. She looks ahead, narrows her eyes.

She's at the bend in the lane. Abby's car is just ahead, tilted on its sunken tire. It's not much of a sanctuary, but it'll do. Case needs a minute . . . or several. She's out of the house, which is something, but now, still radiating with pain, she has to figure out what comes next.

Case jogs forward and reaches for the handle of the passenger-side door. She's sure her luck with unlocked doors has run out for the day, but the handle gives. Case swings the door open, climbs in, and then throws the duffel into the back seat. Her foot hits something hard, and she yelps out in pain. She reaches down, and her hand finds a rock—*the* rock she'd picked up this morning before she crossed the river, when she was *also* convinced she'd have to confront a hog. This is the best weapon yet. Holding the rock, she hauls herself over the center console and into the back seat. Once there, she wedges herself onto the floorboard. Case pushes her duffel bag next to her feet. Her knees are squashed to her chin.

A quick and clever creature of the night, Case is not. She wishes she were.

Shifting awkwardly in the small space, Case pulls the phone from her pocket and cringes when she sees the screen. Only 16 percent battery, and no bars. It's 7:43. Bryan hasn't responded. No one has responded.

And then, to make things even worse, there are sounds approaching from outside the car. They're not the hungry noises hogs make, but the sounds of hushed voices—people being loud-quiet, like Andrea's mom's boyfriend Danny when he used to come home tipsy in the middle of the night. Case tilts her head, like she's tuning in on a radio dial. She picks out Kendall's voice, then Abby's.

"This is your fault," Kendall spits out. "You told her about Charlie. How else would she have known?"

"How is this my fault?" Abby replies. "*I* didn't bring Case here. *I* didn't ask her to come, and I sure as shit didn't tell her that we lured some stranger into a rushing river. You give me no fucking credit, I swear."

"Because you don't deserve any credit!" Kendall barks.

As the voices come closer, Case attempts to wriggle deeper onto the floorboard. Through the window, Case can see the bob of flashlights, proper handheld ones, not the tiny beams from phones. She shouldn't have gotten into this car—she should have just kept going, on foot, down the driveway. She grips the rock in her hand. She will *definitely* hurl it at Kendall before going in for Abby.

"You know what, Kendall?" Abby goes on to say. "Believe what you want. I honestly wouldn't be surprised if one of these days, you come after *me* with a fireplace poker and then tie me up in the cellar, because *clearly* you've turned into a total psychopath."

"Shut up, Abby. You don't get it. You still have family back in Arizona. This place and my sister and Troy are all I have left, and I'll do whatever I can to protect it."

"Wow," Abby drawls. "How brave. Such conviction. Why do you always talk like the main character on some dumb television show?"

"Fuck you." There's a pause, then Kendall's tone shifts. "How much do you think there is?"

"I don't know, sixty bucks maybe."

In the next moment, the front passenger door swings open. Case holds her breath. Abby sticks her head in, releases the catch of the glove box, and starts searching through.

"I usually keep some stashed in here, but it's possible Troy or Andrea found it."

Through the gap between the seat and the door, Case watches as Abby finds something—an envelope—but what the girl does next is strange and stealthy. Abby tosses that envelope behind her, into the back seat, so that it lands on Case's legs and then bounces down to her feet. For a few more seconds, Abby continues to search through the glove box before giving up and slamming it shut. She ducks out of the car and shuts the door.

"It's not here," Case hears Abby say. "There's nothing."

"Crap," Kendall replies. "We're running out of bacon."

Naturally, Kendall would be more concerned about

their bacon supply than about Case, who she clearly still believes is tied up, unconscious, underneath their house.

The loud-hushed voices retreat. Case exhales. And then she waits. Her ankles are kinked at weird angles, and she can feel sweat in the creases of her clothes. Eventually, both of her feet fall asleep. Her head hurts so badly that she can actually *hear* the pain. It goes *whomp, whomp*. Hearing her headache, however, might not be that bad, because now she can't pretend-hear the rooting of the hogs.

Case hazards a glance at her phone: the time shows 7:55. The battery is down to 10 percent.

"Shit," Case mutters.

She grabs the envelope that has fallen to her feet and then turns on the phone's flashlight. A second passes. 9 percent.

It's an envelope addressed to Case in Drea's handwriting. It was once sealed, but now it's been torn open, of course, because one of these shithead roommates went and read it. She rips out the paper and starts reading.

Case!

Do you remember how, when we were kids, we'd sit in your room and look out the window to the house across the street? The same elderly couple had lived there for twenty years or something. We never, _ever_ saw them. They kept their blinds closed and a <u>NO TRESPASSING</u> sign in the window. They had a doghouse but no dog. Once a week, someone would stop by to drop off groceries. A son or a nephew, maybe a volunteer from Meals on Wheels.

There was that addition being built on that house, but it was never finished. There was, like, this paper stuff, with a brand name printed across it, tacked up on the outside of the frame. Strips of siding were supposed to be attached to that, but they never were. The paper had started to fray. The brand name faded as the seasons passed and passed. The house just sat there, unfinished, for years.

You said you were afraid of ending up with a life like that. The kind of life where you looked out your same window and saw that same unfinished house across the street every day, forever. It could've happened. It __had__ happened to people we knew who weren't much older than us. You didn't want to look at a sad, unfinished house, and you didn't want to __be__ a sad, unfinished house.

I feel like that sometimes here, where I'm living now.

I was thinking about all this, and I started writing a story.

Do you remember the hill out here called White Sky? The big one?

I can see it from my window. I think a lot about the witch, and how much you said you wanted to meet her.

So I wrote a story about you, lost on White Sky. Or maybe it's about the both of us. Here it is.

Love you always,

D

WHITE SKY

The shouts came from far away, from the other side of the hill. I wasn't worried. It was going to be a great day. I'd stashed a couple of bottles of water and a box of granola bars in my backpack, so I'd be fine.

Later, in the afternoon, there were still shouts, but there were also whistles. When people go into the woods or on hikes, they're supposed to take whistles with them. If they trip and twist their ankle or fall into a ravine or something, they can blow that whistle, hoping that someone will hear them. The people blowing their whistles must've been hoping that I had one too, and that I'd respond to their whistles with my own. I wasn't going to respond. I didn't have a whistle.

That night, I watched fireworks. They came from the direction of Mineral Wells, and must've been from the homecoming game. I was so high up on the hill that I could look down on the lights soaring up into the sky before they exploded almost directly in front of me. When they rose up, they sounded a little bit like the whistles I'd been hearing all day. I like the fireworks that burst into crackling white sparkles the best.

On the second day, the shouts were louder.

Also, on the second day, I saw the other girl.

I was just sitting, looking over the valley, when I heard the girl say "Hey" from behind me. She asked if I needed help and told me she wasn't one of the people who were out trying to find me. The girl pivoted to the side and said she lived "up there," like, up on the hill. She seemed to me like a girl who took care of herself, with blond hair in a neat ponytail but also layers of dirt on her hands and her wrists and her ankles. She was carrying a thermos covered in faded stickers, and across the front of her cotton button-up shirt was the wide strap of a cross-body bag. She was a girl who set her own priorities and followed her own rules.

"I don't need help," I said.

The girl glanced at my backpack, then frowned.

"I'll check back later maybe."

The next day, the girl came back.

"Come on." Along with her thermos and her messenger bag, she was carrying a fishing rod over her shoulder, and an old plastic bucket. "Bring your pack. Let's go to the river."

A part of me wanted to tell her again that I didn't need her help, but I was hungry and getting lonely. The night before had been cold. I swore I heard the baying of coyotes. I'd barely slept.

On the way down the hill, I tripped on an exposed root and fell. It was an ugly fall, one that threw me first into the trunk of a tree, then down to the rocky soil. The girl helped me up. The skin on her hand, as it wrapped around my wrist, felt wrinkled, and almost too moist. She asked if I was okay, and I said I was, which wasn't completely true.

At the river, we took turns trying to catch fish. The girl didn't ask, but I told her some of the reasons why I left home. My mom was having a hard time making ends meet. My period was so bad that every month I got migraines and threw up. My grades were getting worse, across the board, in every class. My brain wasn't processing information. It wasn't working right.

The girl listened but didn't say much. When she talked, it was about the river, the hill, the sky, and the animals. _This_ was the world she lived in. I told her about the coyotes, and she said there were more around than there used to be, and that I should watch out for them.

"Did you bring a knife?" she asked. "You should've brought a knife."

The girl pointed to the sky and said that big white birds were migrating in, ones she'd never seen before. Seabirds, she called them. But why would seabirds come so far inland?

As she stood, ankle-deep in the water, she hummed songs that I thought sounded familiar, but when I try to remember them now, I can't.

Standing in the river, humming her songs, was when the girl looked the blurriest. I think it had to do with how the sun was lighting her up from behind as it rose over the water. It chiseled out her deep silhouette. She plucked a white flower from the bank and gave it to me.

She told me that the earth was angry, that something would happen soon. I believed her but didn't believe her. I was at a point in my life where I believed anything could happen. Nothing would surprise me, wonderful or terrible.

We caught three fish that day, trudged back up the hill, and cooked them by a fire the girl started by herself. That night, I didn't hear shouts from the people who were out looking for me, but I did hear the coyotes again.

The next morning was the worst. There were flies everywhere. They must've been attracted to the salt on my skin or the smell of cooked fish on my fingers. The flower the girl had picked was next to me, on top of my backpack. The white was still so white.

I had a home—a house. I couldn't see it from where I was on the side of the hill, but I knew where it was. Out _there_ somewhere. I didn't belong at that house. There are some places that only serve as reminders of where you _don't_ belong.

While I ate my last granola bar, I imagined the people who would finally come to find me. They'd be happy. They'd have water and snacks. They'd urge me to sit down and rest, even though I wouldn't be very tired. They may have a dog with them, a friendly brown Lab, living its best life on a rescue mission.

"Your mother misses you," they'd say.

I'd look beyond those people and their dog, into the trees, where the girl would be standing, half merged with the shadows. Would she look disappointed? Had she wanted me to stay?

"Your mother misses you," the people would say again, thinking I didn't hear them the first time.

I would eventually go with those people, but I would never be the same.

EIGHT THIRTY

ONE MIGHT THINK, after all that's happened, that Case wouldn't put much faith in strangers, and that jogging along the edge of the highway with her left arm extended and her thumb pointing upward, hoping to hitch a ride into town, might be a bad idea. But until today, Case has typically had good luck with strangers. She trusts them, though she doesn't know exactly why. It might be because Case's own mother, who is supposed to be the most trusted person in her life, is so *not* trustworthy. It might also be because, for Case, strangers have always emerged to help her at just the right time.

Andrea was once a stranger who'd emerged to help Case at just the right time. Case was twelve and walking to Timmy's to pick up snacks for Walter. It was dusk, during summer, and Case was taking her time, because she knew Walter wanted her gone for as long as possible. For a while, she sat in a shady spot, near a row of old crape myrtles that lined a ditch everyone in town optimistically referred to as a creek. Once she left there, she passed by an abandoned house, but first she stopped to peer through its dirty windows, spying a floor littered with empty pizza boxes, crushed cans, and a couple of old sleeping bags. Outside the community center, she read the notices on the bulletin board, which mostly had to do with tryouts for the upcoming football season.

When the store was in sight, she passed a group of older boys from the junior high playing basketball in a driveway. Case walked a little faster.

"Case!" one of them called out. "Hey, Case! Come be on *my* team!"

They knew her name because everyone knew everyone. Case didn't look, didn't break stride.

"Yeah, come *play* with us," another added.

Case had always been leggy. When she was a kid, she was *gangly*, but now she was *lithe*. She'd hit a growth spurt the spring before, and was wearing a tank top and her favorite pair of purple athletic shorts. She'd outgrown both. With the acorn-brown tan she achieved during the summers, she resembled her grandfather, who she knew lived somewhere in the southern part of New Mexico.

The bounce of the basketball slowed, then stopped. Case watched those boys out of the corner of her eye and moved those leggy legs of hers faster.

Once inside Timmy's, Case dawdled, let the icy air-conditioning bite at her bare skin. She knew what she was going to buy for Walter, but she pretended like she didn't, pretended like she had choices. At some point a long time ago, Case had developed a silly fantasy. Years from now, after she left Palo Pinto County, graduated from college, and landed some cool job, she'd come back here to Timmy's and buy whatever she wanted, whatever her fingers brushed across as she sauntered down the aisles—five bags of cherry sours, a plastic funnel and some motor oil, a whole tub of cheddar puffs, kiwi-flavored wine coolers. Compared to other fantasies, it wasn't particularly ambitious, but at the time, it was all Case had.

When Case left Timmy's with a couple of bags of potato chips and a chocolate bar that would most certainly melt before Case got back to her house, the boys were still out playing basketball, so Case decided to try a different way home. It was darker now, but the ground was still hot, radiant from the day. Case cut between houses and went down an unpaved side street. All around, the yard dogs seemed more agitated than normal. They were launching themselves against their chain-link fences and tugging at their tethers. At first, Case thought their behavior was due to the twilight, when the shadows stretch long and the dogs have gotten tired of waiting for their food all day. But that wasn't it.

Hogs mostly live in the woods, but that doesn't stop them from wandering out and into the neighborhoods. They lack both fear of humans and a sense of self-preservation, and if they're awake, they're hungry. The dusk is when they shake off sleep, and when they start to look for something to eat.

And, yes, Case heard the hog before she saw it. There was a grunt—different from a dog's. The sound was wetter, from way up in the snout. There was a quick shuffle, then the hard ring of something metal being bumped into. Case stopped walking and watched the hog emerge from between a couple of large trash bins. At first, it didn't see Case. Its head was down. Its snout was roving across the ground, and Case could make out the tip of its tusk shoving out the side of its mouth. A front hoof was digging around at spilled bits of trash. The hog's bloated body was black. It was scarred and missing strips of hair.

Stuck in their yards, the dogs were going nuts.

Case nervously adjusted her grip on the plastic Timmy's bag, and that faint rustle was enough to snag the hog's attention. It didn't even pause to size her up before it charged. Case ran, bolting between houses to get closer to the main road, where she knew there would be more people. Even the boys playing basketball would've been a welcome sight. She needed help, or she needed the hog to fixate on someone or something else.

Case ran and ran, but no matter how quick she was, she couldn't shake the animal. Behind her, the hog was snarling, loping forward. The main road seemed so far away. The cars passed by in the distance, their windshields lit up golden by the sunset.

"Hey!"

Case heard the girl call out from ahead. She was standing on her porch, leaning over the rail and waving her whole arm side to side.

"Hey, over here!" the girl yelled. "Come inside!"

Case bolted toward the girl, who was only a couple houses away, and as she came closer, the girl stopped waving and held her arm out straight. Case thought she was holding a pistol, and, on instinct, she flinched and nearly stumbled. Quickly, though, she righted herself and kept running, dashing up the porch steps. The girl was going to kill the hog, Case figured, and Case was grateful for her unexpected hero.

As Case flew by, the girl squeezed the trigger. But it wasn't a gun she'd been holding. It was an air horn—the kind people sound off during football games.

Case yelped and spun around in the doorway to see the startled hog fall back on its stubby hind legs. The girl took a step off the porch and, with a frown, blew the horn again, longer this time. The hog snorted, then paused. It raked one of its hooves through the dying grass of the yard and went loping off down the street in the opposite direction.

"That was scary," the girl said to Case, who was collapsed against the doorframe, panting. "Do you want a Coke?"

The girl moved without waiting for Case to answer, and eventually, once Case caught her breath, she followed the girl inside. The house smelled like fresh paint, and was full of moving boxes.

"I'm glad I saw you," the girl went on to say. "I'm Andrea." She handed Case a can of Coke from the long cardboard box on the counter. "Sorry it's not cold. We just moved in. The electric's not on yet."

"How did you know that would work?" Case asked. "The air horn."

"I didn't," Andrea replied, popping open a warm soda. "But I had to try *something*. Lucky guess, right?"

Later that night, when Case finally got back to her house, she apologized to Walter for being late. He looked up at her from his spot on the couch, his toothpick spinning between his teeth. He seemed confused, like he'd forgotten she'd been gone in the first place.

Now, years later, the person to emerge at just the right time is Bryan Jennison. And, once again, Case is running down a road in Palo Pinto County, this time with both straps of her duffel hooked over her shoulders like a backpack. With her nonhitchhiking hand, she pulls out her phone to check the time. Just as she reads that it's 8:30, headlights illuminate her from behind. She can hear tires shift from the gritty road to the grittier shoulder and then come to a complete stop. Case slows, drops her arm, and turns to watch Bryan step out from his pickup truck. He leaves the door open and the engine running.

"Case!" he exclaims. "Hey! It's you." Bryan pauses, then points. "Are you okay?"

"No," Case pants, slumping over and bracing her hands against her knees. "Not okay. You got my text?"

"No." Bryan shakes his head. "I was on my lunch break, headed home to pick up a clean shirt before going right back. I'm sorry if you tried sending me something. Sometimes calls don't connect out here." He takes a couple steps closer, then stops. "What's that rope for?"

Case doesn't really know how to answer that question,

but she does know that whatever she says next will probably sound completely bonkers.

"They hit me." She pauses to gulp more air into her burning lungs. "Tied me up. I think they killed someone."

"*What*? Andrea Soto?"

"No. Well . . . Yes, probably."

It's a safe assumption. The only thing that makes sense in this nonsense place. What Case knows for sure is what Drea wrote—she was going down to the river with her housemates and with Charlie. After that, no more Drea. No more Drea's writing.

Case's heart is beating so fast in her chest it hurts. It's beating, and it's breaking.

"Drea's dead. They killed her."

Bryan steps closer. "Have you called the sheriff?"

"Can't. No reception."

"I can take you to town," Bryan offers, gesturing to his truck. "That's where you're headed, right?"

Case is still bent double, but she manages to straighten up enough to look at Bryan. The lights on this road are few and far between. There isn't one near them, so Bryan is just a shadow person against a shadow truck on a shadow road, sort of blurry at the edges like the stranger girl in Drea's story.

This is all so hard. All of these stories—old, new, real, fiction—are overlapping in Case's overstretched brain. She doesn't know how to pull the stories apart and sort them into the correct order. She can't interpret anything right now.

Case desperately wants to trust Bryan. He's from around here, and that goes a long way. Also, and most important, Bryan has been checking up on her, making sure she's okay. Now, he's offering his help, and she wants to take it.

"Are you going to try and throw me in the river?" Case asks, still breathless.

Bryan laughs awkwardly, not really sure if Case is joking or not. "I, uh, wasn't planning on it."

"Do you have any Advil in your truck?" Case says. "Or Tylenol or anything?"

"I think so, yeah. Advil."

"Great," Case replies. She shrugs the straps of her duffel from her shoulders and lets the bag fall heavy into one hand. "Let's go."

NINE TWELVE

HERE IS A TRUCK, brakes squealing as it skids to a stop outside of the station. Here are the doors of that truck flying open before the engine is even off, followed by two kids hustling into the station. One of those kids is Bryan, who the deputy immediately recognizes from the Timmy's in Millsap, and the other is that girl from the news a couple of years ago—the one from around here that got burned, nearly died, in a house fire. The deputy remembers her face, and can also see the scars up and down her right arm from where she has her sleeve rolled up. That was a big story back in the day. The girl's scars trigger another memory— of the man who set that fire, some drunk asshole who was pissed he got dumped by his woman and was now serving time at the federal penitentiary in Huntsville.

The girl pulls out a bunch of papers from her pocket, but as she does that, some other stuff falls out, too: a lighter, a book of matches, a folding knife. She doesn't stoop to pick any of that stuff up. Bryan does that for her. The girl just spreads out all these crumpled pieces of paper and starts pointing and talking real fast. She says something about a house near the river, strangers who are camped out there, a local girl named Andrea, a nonlocal boy named Charlie. Then she points to her head, to a bump near her eye.

"I mean, look at me," the girl says. "Do you think I would've done this to *myself*?"

The deputy then turns to ask Bryan, "Is this for real?"

When Bryan says yes without even hesitating, the girl practically buckles with gratitude.

"What is your name, young lady?" the deputy asks.

"Case Lopez," the girl replies.

That's right, the deputy remembers. *Case.* An uncommon name.

"Something happened to my friend." The girl—Case—stabs her finger against one of the pieces of paper. "Please. You have to go out there. You also need to find her mother. Gloria Soto. She used to live around here. She still might."

"Did you actually see something happen?" the deputy asks. "Did someone get hurt?"

"Please." This time Case spreads her palm flat on the pages and slides them across the counter. "Just read it."

After about twenty minutes, the deputy has finished reading and is sorting all of Andrea's pages into a neat stack. Case and Bryan wait together on a nearby bench. Case's leg is bouncing impatiently as she tries and fails to read the deputy's facial expressions. She wants him to say something, but she also wants those papers back. Just as she's about to stand and demand the return of Andrea's writing,

Case's vision does something glitchy. In the attempt to straighten things out, she jams her thumbs into the ridges above both eyebrows.

"Are you all right?" Bryan asks. Then, almost immediately: "Of course you're not all right. You want another Advil?"

On the drive here, Case took two from the bottle Bryan had stashed in his glove box, but a third might help.

"Maybe, yeah."

As Bryan steps out the door, the deputy clears his throat. Case snaps to attention.

"I'm the only one here tonight," he says, "so I can't leave the station, but I'll put in a call to the other deputy on duty, and she'll try and make it out there when she can. We've had a lot of calls come in tonight, though, so it might be a while." He flashes a polite grin. "It's been a busy night in Palo Pinto County."

Case waits for more. For a reaction to all the wild shit detailed on those pages. For anything.

"That's it?" Case asks finally. "That's a joke, right? A busy night in Palo Pinto County?"

"Like I said, my colleague will try and make it out there," the deputy repeats. "If this is true, then, yes, it's worth looking into."

"It *is* true," Case snaps. "And after I told those people out there that I knew it was true, one of them hit me over the head with a blunt object, so . . ." She points to her head again.

"Okay, like I said—we'll look into it."

That's not what he just said, though. He said—*twice*—that they would "try and make it out there." Case grunts. She should've left that oil-soaked rag on the gas stove and burned the house down.

"Can I have those papers back, please?"

"We'll need to keep these," the deputy says. "For evidence."

For a split second, Case entertains the idea of pushing past the deputy and swiping the journal pages off his desk, but then Bryan returns. Case can hear the tiny rattle of the Advil bottle in Bryan's hand. She stops short and is disappointed in how much she instinctively responds to the sound of pills against plastic.

"What's going on?" Bryan asks.

"We're leaving," Case says.

Once they're in the car, Case takes the Advil from Bryan and shakes out two into her hand.

"What next?" Bryan asks.

Case makes a half turn in the passenger seat, pointing past Bryan out the window and into the far distance, to the largest hill in the county, the one with the stories.

"Over there," Case says. "I want to go to White Sky."

TEN TWENTY

THERE'S NO REAL PLAN HERE. Case is walking. Bryan is behind her, keeping up at a steady pace, though he keeps coughing into his sleeve, which makes Case think he's pretending to hide the fact that he's bothered by the bad air. There are no trails on White Sky, but there are some open spots, small clearings that are full of grass that has died and been flattened into swirls. Mostly, though, there are trees. Trees and more trees. There are fresh scrapes on Case's face from the branches on all the trees—a particularly nasty one on her left eyelid—and snapped-off twigs are snagged in her hair.

As Case walks, she swings her flashlight across the ground, hoping the beam will land on a dirty foot, a discarded crown of ivy, a thermos covered with stickers. At least now she has a real flashlight, which she got from Bryan, and isn't forced to rely on the paltry beam from her perpetually dying phone. Small bugs swarm around her hand, attracted by the light.

Every so often, from behind her, the beam from Bryan's flashlight lands at Case's feet, then bounces away.

"It might rain," Bryan says.

"Maybe," Case replies distractedly.

"There's something in the wind," Bryan goes on to say.

Case doesn't even have to look up to know he's right. For the most part, the air up here is still and thick, with occasional little punches of cold coming through. It's those cold punches that seem to hold something, like warnings. In addition to the lights from town, Case can see the occasional burst of lightning in the western sky—not the scary kind, not long, thin jagged bolts, but the gentler kind, farther away and hidden behind dense clouds. Every so often, sections of the sky bloom with light. It's beautiful, but also eerie. Something's building up in there.

"Where did you move to?" Bryan asks. "When you left Palo Pinto? It's like one day you were at school, and the next, you weren't."

"Fort Worth. We moved to there so my mom could be with her sister," Case says. She brushes loose strands of hair away from her face. The reason they suddenly feel sticky against her skin must be from the lightning, causing static to build in the air. "When I saw you back at Timmy's it seemed like you didn't recognize me."

"I knew who you were," Bryan says.

"I didn't want to come back. The only reason I ever did was to see Drea."

"Is it really *that* bad?" Bryan asks. "Palo Pinto?"

Case sighs. "You'll think I'm exaggerating, but I've always had the sense this place was out to destroy me. And then, with the fire, that almost happened. I moved away. I felt marginally better. I made the decision to move farther away for college, and felt way, *way* better. I came back today, just one last time, to see the most important person in my life, and Palo Pinto County is trying to destroy me again. And I'm pretty sure it succeeded in destroying Drea. So, yeah, it is *that* bad." Case pauses. "But, then, sometimes I love it. I don't know. It's complicated."

"Okay," Bryan says. "That sounds reasonable."

Case snorts.

"I still don't get why Andrea was out here with those kids, though," Bryan continues. "Why wasn't she spending the summer break with her mom? You mentioned back at the store that they used to live on Old Millsap Road."

"She came out here in the spring, right after Pilot Knob," Case says. "That all happened really close to her school. Everyone was forced to evacuate, and a guy she knew was headed to a house out here that his family owns. She wrote me letters about it. The trip up here was apparently pretty hard."

Pretty hard. Right.

Case thinks about the nameless boy Drea mentioned in her journal entry—the one Abby ran over simply because he was persistent about wanting water. What happened to him was one of probably thousands of examples of trage-dies that unfolded every day for weeks. Exposure to those tragedies was unavoidable. The awful news came in quickly and never stopped.

Pilot Knob, a supposedly dormant volcano tucked into the hills south of Austin, had been secretly churning back to life. There were warnings, and a few panicked scientists who appeared on the news, but they weren't taken seriously. It was like a possible volcanic eruption ranked low on everyone's list of terrible things to be on the lookout for.

One day last April, however, Pilot Knob finally popped. For three whole days, ash and chunks of rock flew into the air. The airport was wiped out, the runways pummeled, and the interstate that stretched from Austin to San Antonio was immediately rendered completely unusable. Evacuations were ordered, but many people didn't really know where to go, or how to get there. Case remembers the pictures snapped from helicopters by photographers who braved flying through the gray sky. They captured video of miles-long lines of cars, some of them abandoned; campfires burning at tent cities set up on the sides of highways; people marching on foot. She also remembers the clips people took themselves and uploaded online. There were pleas for food, water, and gas, along with links to GoFundMe pages; video of people smashing car windows and searching for anything of value inside; audio of multiple home alarms chirping up and down one darkened street. In the days that followed, there were telethons, fundraisers, bake sales, blood drives—all featuring stories about lives that had been immeasurably altered for the worst.

Case watched it all unfold, every day, on her phone. Every day, it was like the entire spectrum of human tragedy played out right there in her hand. Andrea had lived through that mass evacuation and the long, slow drive northward, and had somehow still managed to find joy in things like bread and an old pair of boots found in the woods.

Even from almost two hundred miles away, up in Fort Worth, the skies had darkened, turned the color of fruit punch. One day, in early May, everyone had walked out of Case's school at the final bell to find the parking lot covered in black birds, which had died in the sky and fallen to the ground. Her friends were forced to flick feathered carcasses off their windshields, and listen to tiny bones snap as they backed their cars out of their parking spaces.

"Man, those stories," Bryan begins.

Case stops walking and turns, thinking she and Bryan are on the same wavelength, that he's about to recall his own story from the tragedy spectrum.

"I saw something once about a group of people helping deliver a baby. The mother's car was stalled out on one of the farm roads. There were, like, five or six people who pulled over to help with the birth, and after that, someone with a four-wheeler volunteered to take the woman and her newborn to the nearest clinic."

Bryan's flashlight is giving out. The beam has started to flicker. Case hears Bryan give it a couple sharp whacks on the side, trying to shove the battery connection straight.

"Even up here in Palo Pinto," Bryan goes on to say, "Timmy's ran out of gas a few times and the shelves got pretty bare, but Linda was adamant—we were going to stay open for the people coming through. She got her husband to hitch up their smoker to his truck and bring it from their house to the store, and together they cooked all kinds of stuff. Like, day and night, for weeks. Even on the days the weather got really bad, we were all still out there, grilling corn and burgers, cutting up bars of soap so people could tidy up in our little bathroom, helping out any way we could."

"I think you're similar," Case says after a moment. "You and Drea."

Bryan chuckles. "How so?"

"She wrote me a story. It was about a girl who came up here to White Sky because she was running away from something bad at home. Someone who lived up here found her and helped her. Drea liked stories about people looking out for each other."

"So you think that story was about *her*," Bryan says.

"I don't know," Case says in a rush. "That's the problem. I just don't *know*. I mean, she *told* me to come out here to visit. She gave me directions to a house, but she wasn't there. I soon realized that all of her stuff was gone except for these totally cryptic journal entries that possibly describe the lead-up to a *murder*. And when I confronted her roommates about it, one of them knocked me out with a fireplace poker. *And* when I somehow recovered from *that*, another one of the roommates secretly passed me a story Drea wrote about running away to White Sky. So does that *mean* something?"

Bryan coughs again. The sound of his gnarly hacking makes Case pause and check her phone. It's 10:20.

"You know," Bryan says. "I've actually been up here before. It was a dare. There's a story about this place. There's a ghost."

"Not a ghost," Case says. "A witch."

"That's not how I heard it. It's a ghost—the ghost of a woman who got lost and then died. Hey, Case," Bryan says, stopping. "Look at this."

Case spins around. Bryan's still-flickering light has landed on a piece of pink cloth on the ground, and when Case crouches to get a better look, she can clearly see something that's been shoved in the underbrush. Her own flashlight beam lands on a zipper, then a couple of faded patches, then a recognizable logo. Altogether, it's a backpack.

Case dives toward the bag, which gapes open when she tugs it toward her.

"Drea." Case's voice, after more than twelve hours of saying the same name, has started to give out. It breaks on the last, weak syllable.

The inside of the backpack is empty except for some dead leaves and a single corroded battery, and there are black dots of mildew all across the front pocket. The pack itself is made of nylon, which is brittle from being out in the elements for so long. Little strands of fabric break off between Case's fingers. This thing is *old*. Case searches the inner compartments anyway, for anything, holding the flashlight awkwardly between her chin and her chest so she can dig through it with both her hands.

There's nothing there, though. The pack is so empty Case wonders if it's been found and rifled through before. She shoves her hand into one of the side pockets, and that's when she finally finds something. At first, she thinks it's a note card, but when she pulls harder, the card comes free, sort of. It's not a note card, but a tag, connected to the bag. It's the kind of tag someone keeps on their luggage, with their name and contact information on it.

Case regrips her flashlight to get a better angle of light, and can see that this bag does not somehow magically belong to Andrea Soto but to someone named Lucy Barris. There's also an address in Eastland, which is a town a few miles to the west of here, down the interstate.

Here, Case thinks, *is another girl gone, reduced to scraps and handwriting.* She lifts the tag so Bryan can read the name.

"We can take it with us," Bryan says. "Maybe give it to the sheriff."

"Sure." Case huffs out a breath. "Another mystery they won't solve."

"Case," Bryan says gently, "I don't think she's here."

"I know," Case snaps. "I know that."

"The thing I don't get the most," Bryan continues, "is why you're trying to figure all this out alone. I realize Andrea is important to you, but why are *we* the ones tramping up White Sky in the middle of the night? The sheriff's office can figure this out way better than we can."

Case presses the palm of her hand into her forehead and mashes it around in the attempt to flatten out her lingering headache. She's also doing this instead of letting out the most primal scream ever.

Case is *not* normal. That was such a lie. Despite the hours and hours of therapy and the many, many hot baths, her anger is still here. It hasn't gone away—hasn't dissolved into the bath or been sucked down any drain. It may have been buried, for a while, but everything that's happened in these last twelve or whatever hours has helped to push it right back to the surface.

"The *sheriff*?" Case says. "Are you kidding me, Bryan. Andrea is *the most* important person in my life, and the sheriff's office just proved they don't give a shit. They barely even believe any of this is real. *This* is why I'm tramping up White Sky in the middle of the night—because I have to do *something*. I can't just do *nothing*. Does that not make sense to you?"

Bryan is listening—he's trying to take in all of Case's mad logic and process it, but Case isn't convinced he gets it. He must not have an Andrea in his life, so he can't really know what Case is talking about. Or maybe that's wrong. Maybe he has multiple Andreas, a whole host of people who would try to pull him out of a burning building, who would stand down a wild animal for him. If that's the case, then maybe the prospect of losing only one of those people wouldn't cause him to plow through trees and trip across rocks in the dead of night, searching for the ghost of a ghost.

Just when Case's mounting anger is about to take over and she's about to say something rude, like *You don't fucking understand*, Bryan hits the side of his flashlight. The beam steadies out, and he points it up the hill. Then he takes a big breath in, and the cough that follows is lighter, not as severe as before.

"Lead the way," he says.

"The air," Case says. "It's making you sick."

"It's fine. I'm used to it. Let's keep walking."

Case has the strangest urge to throw her arms around Bryan, take his shirt in between her teeth, and hold on to this precious, new stranger forever. She won't do that, though. Instead, she gives him the gift of a secret.

"Ever since I was a kid," Case says, "I've wanted to get lost on White Sky."

"Does tonight count as getting lost?" Bryan asks.

"I think so," Case says. "But more than anything, I wanted to come down from White Sky as a different person."

"Maybe that's what happened to Lucy Barris," Bryan offers.

"Maybe, yeah." Case turns to point the beam of her flashlight back down the hill. "Thank you for trudging up a small mountain in the middle of the night with me."

"That's it, then?" Bryan asks. "We're done? We'll just wait for the sheriff?"

"Oh, *hell* no," Case says. "We're going back to that house. I've decided that if there *are* things out to destroy me tonight in Palo Pinto County, then I'm going to face them head-on."

"Oh, that's the spirit," Bryan says. "And if you get in any trouble, at least you're armed with an old pocketknife."

Case laughs. "Don't underestimate me, all right? I also have some rope. And a lighter. I'm sure I'll be fine."

TEN FIFTY-SEVEN

"YOUR HEADACHE ANY BETTER?"

Bryan starts his truck, eases it off the shoulder and onto the road. The clock on the dashboard reads 10:57.

"Maybe a little," Case replies. As the truck picks up speed, she keeps her eye on the edges of the dark road. Lucy Barris's backpack is in her lap, and her own duffel bag is wedged between her feet on the floorboard. "The headaches are a side effect from all my surgeries. I carry a prescription wherever I go, but my pills were stolen back at the house."

Bryan looks over, raising his eyebrows. "I wasn't judging you, Case."

"I know. I just don't like being this person who has to take pills all the time. It makes me feel like I'm . . . deficient."

"You also just suffered a concussion, apparently, at the hands of some awful people," Bryan offers dryly. "So I think you get a pass tonight."

"There *is* that." Case pauses. "Thanks for everything," she adds. "Sending those texts. Stopping when I was out on the road."

"No problem," Bryan says. "I was just driving around anyway."

Case looks across the cabin of the truck and bursts out laughing.

"What?" Bryan says, grinning. "I like to drive around on my lunch break. Is that weird?"

"No, it's not weird. It's just that your lunch break probably ended, like, two hours ago, and now you're going to get fired. I thought you said you were going home for a new shirt."

"First of all, I'm *not* going to get fired," Bryan says. "You might not believe this, but not many people are lining up to work double shifts at Timmy's. Second, I *did* need a new shirt. I was just taking my time getting back to the store."

The truck passes onto the trestle bridge that crosses the Brazos, causing the tires to bump and rattle over the uneven surface.

"I need to tell you something," Case begins. "I once pushed someone down a set of stadium stairs."

"Okay," Bryan says. "Was it . . . on purpose?"

"Uh, can something be both an accident and on purpose?" Case asks. She goes on before Bryan can respond. "Anyway, I just wanted you to know. I'm aware that I've mentioned that the roommates back at the house are totally shitty people, but I'm not that great, either."

In the same moment Case hears Bryan tell her to "Get real," she sees something—a flutter in the dark, darting across the windshield, from right to left.

It's so close that Bryan flinches and taps on the brakes. "Did you see that?" he asks. "Was that a bird?"

In the same moment he leans forward over the steering wheel to try to get a better look, his side window shatters.

The truck immediately goes into a spin, and Case is yanked hard to the side. Out of the corner of her eye, she can see Bryan's hands, passing over and over each other on the steering wheel as he tries to keep control. He's steering into the spin, which you're supposed to do, but it doesn't seem to be helping. Case ducks down, covers her head, and closes her eyes. She smells rubber, hears the scream of brakes. She also hears small clicks and, again, for the second time in a day, the awful sound of wings beating in a space where wings shouldn't beat. There's something in here in the truck with them. On instinct, Case reaches for her duffel and wedges it up against her stomach.

This is it. Case is fully expecting to finally be destroyed. It could be by the sharp talons of a confused bird of prey, or the impact of the truck against the guardrail, or the dark river below once the truck plummets into it. Then the truck stops so suddenly Case is thrown forward against her seat belt, then back against the seat. Her head hits the relative softness of a cloth-covered headrest. But her skull rings.

Case hazards a glance. The truck is alone on the bridge, and by the glow of the headlights, she can see it has turned in a perfect circle. Bryan's hands are still gripping the wheel at ten and two, but now his forehead is pressed against the wheel between them. Case can see the back of his rib cage rising and falling as he tries to sort out his breathing. The window on the other side of him is gone. It was rolled up when they were driving. Now there are just some stray crystals clinging to the empty frame.

There's no bird, but there are feathers—at least five, half as long as Case's forearm, their colors a collage of earth tones. The leather of the seat behind Bryan has been flayed open, but Bryan himself seems okay. Case scans the back of his neck, his shirt, the exposed skin of his hands. From what she can see, he's not bleeding.

"Was that a bird?" Bryan asks again, not lifting his head. "Is it gone?"

"It's gone, yeah," Case says. She feels queasy and claustrophobic. "Something like this happened earlier. At the house. Two hawks flew in. They destroyed an entire room."

Bryan turns his head. "Why would they do that?"

"I don't know," Case replies. But she does know, or she has an idea: fire, flood, being set upon by animals. Does this mean Case has the bad luck of being targeted or the good luck of being spared?

Case tries her door, which opens a few inches before hitting the guardrail. It takes some fancy contorting, but Case manages to squeeze through the small opening. Once out of the truck, she can hear the river. It's far, far below the bridge, but it's loud. Case leans over the rail, but she can't see much—just the occasional white crest water makes when it suddenly changes course or hits rock.

"They must've opened the dam again."

Case pivots. Bryan has stepped from the truck and is passing through the headlight beams, making his way around toward her.

"From Possum Kingdom," he adds.

"Did this happen before?" Case asks. "Like, a week ago?"

"I think so, yeah. A couple of big storms passed through recently, and the lake levels got too high too fast."

"C'mon," Case urges, moving back toward the truck again. "Let's keep going."

"We can't." Bryan points to the tires. The one on the front passenger side is flat from the collision with the guardrail. "I can put on the spare, but it'll take me a few minutes."

"It's fine," Case says, already setting off at a jog. "I'll run. Just meet me there. Don't lose those bags!"

ELEVEN THIRTY

CASE KNOWS WHERE SHE IS, knows where to turn off the road and onto the driveway because she sees the coyote pup strung up on the half-fallen fence. Its puffy tail rests on the ground. Its nose, pointed toward the sky, is framed by its forepaws.

Poor thing. Killed because of its natural instincts. Displayed pitifully as a warning. Case tries not to look at it as she passes, but she can't help but stare.

When she's about a hundred yards down the lane she slows her pace and checks the time on her phone: 11:30 p.m. She's winded but not exhausted. Whenever Case runs, she can't hear all that well. When she runs, she hears her breath and the churn of the blood in her body, but right now she wants to hear the woods, and the sounds that surround the lane. This is different from before, when she was escaping and trying to ignore the sounds of creatures lurking in the night.

Case takes the pocketknife from her jeans, flips the blade free, and grips the handle tight. If something—human or animal—comes for her, she might lose the fight, but at least she'll be able to get in one good swipe.

The lane feels longer than before, but that's probably because her strides are shorter, more careful as she navigates the dark and gritty terrain. There's no SUV belonging to a sheriff's deputy parked anywhere, and Case isn't surprised. She steps on something hard, then reaches down to search the ground. Her fingers find the screwdriver she dropped earlier. Good: another little weapon. She shoves it into her pocket, and then heads to Abby's car, which is still tilted and abandoned.

As she approaches, Case hears two sounds: a breath and a step. She swoops into a crouch and huddles behind the back bumper. From here, the license plate is directly in her line of sight, and she works to commit the number-letter combination to memory, just in case.

"BH679. BH679," she repeats to herself while spinning the handle of the knife in her hand.

There's another breath—an exhale, followed by a dry cough—followed by more steps. Then, instead of hearing something else, Case smells something, strong and unmistakable: a blend of pine-scented chemicals and expensive perfume. She straightens and walks into the lane, and into the beam of a flashlight.

"Oh," Abby says. "There you are. We've been looking for you."

Her tone is flat, practically blasé. She actually seems to be chewing gum.

Here is Case, armed with a blade and her awesome anger, ready to be a badass. Abby, though, somehow has a talent for sucking the emotional energy out of every situation.

"Have you been out here the whole time?" Abby asks.

It takes everything Case has not to roll her eyes. Instead, she steps forward, straight into Abby's cloud of fake scents. "I need you to tell me what happened," she says.

Abby stands there thinking, smacking her gum.

"Fine," she says eventually. "Get in the car."

Abby reaches for the driver's-side door handle, but then pauses when she notices Case hasn't moved.

"I'm not going to do anything to you," Abby says. She holds up her non-flashlight hand. "I don't have anything to hurt you with. I just don't want to talk about this out in the open."

Case relents, opens the passenger door, and slides in beside Abby. Because the car is tilted on its back flat tire, Case is sort of pinned by gravity against the door, and has to look up toward Abby at a weird angle.

"Sometimes," Abby says, clicking off her flashlight, "after running errands, I park out here in the lane and sit by myself for a while. I like having my own space."

"Wow, that's really great," Case drawls. "Now tell me what happened."

"We didn't kill Charlie," Abby says, pivoting in her seat to look at Case. "We didn't have to. He saw the water was too high and moving too fast, and he just waded right in. He said he wanted to be in the water. We didn't push him in, but we didn't try to stop him, either. Except for Andrea.

She was the only one who warned him about the current. She was pointing to something upstream, telling Charlie to move. It must've been a piece of wood or, like, a part of a tree. I couldn't see it, but it came up really fast and hit Charlie, and he went under. After a few seconds, he burst back up and started reaching for the bank, for us, where we were standing. Drea went in after him, but when he grabbed for her, she slipped, and he ended up pulling her in, too. After that, they were both gone. It all happened in less than a minute."

Abby leans in. The inside of the car is pitch black, but Case can still see the shine of Abby's near-white hair. Some of the strands reach down and rest on Case's sleeve.

"Now tell me, Case," Abby says. "Am I lying? You knew Andrea better than anyone. Does that sound like something she would do? Wade into a river to help a stranger?"

"Absolutely," Case replies. "All of it."

Abby sighs, then sits back in her seat. "Go ahead." She gestures to the knife in Case's hand. "Stab me. I know you want to—even though I've been helping you all day. I unlocked the door to Drea's room. I left your phone out in the kitchen, under a light, where you could find it. I gave you that letter from my car . . ."

"You kept me locked up and tied up in the cellar," Case adds. "You'll forgive me if I can't find it in my heart to thank you for doing *way* less than the bare minimum."

Abby scoffs. "What I've been *trying* to tell you, since you haven't noticed by now, is that I'm *lazy*. You totally should've noticed, because I'm the one who tied you to that chair. A half-hearted effort, like most of the things I do."

"You know what?" Case says, reaching for the door handle. "Fuck this."

"Wait, listen," Abby says. She reaches out to grab Case by her sleeve. The pointer finger of her other hand is hovering in front of Case's lips. "I'm going to do you one more favor. Troy and Kendall are down by the river. I'm heading out there next, but I'll pretend like I didn't see you just now. They know you're gone, and they think that maybe you're searching around for Drea. You sure scared the shit out of them when you mentioned Charlie. I don't know how you knew about that, but well played. You can surprise them, give 'em a little . . ." Abby makes a shoving motion with both her hands.

Abby smirks, the devil. And Case has to admit: she's considering it.

"Earlier," Case says, "when the two of you were in the lane, Kendall mentioned not having anyone left. What did she mean by that?"

"They died," Abby says. "Right when they heard about the eruption, her and Steph's parents tried to drive from Houston to Austin, but the winds were blowing ash everywhere and the air was too thick. They were part of a big wreck on the highway. We didn't hear about it until we were already up here, at which point Kendall went and threw her phone in the river and married the house."

A bolt of empathy hits Case right in the gut. Kendall had

suffered a tragedy on top of a tragedy, and was trying to cope in whatever way possible. Case knew what that was like.

"You said Troy and Kendall were over by the river?" Case asks.

Abby nods.

"Steph is at the house, though?"

Abby looks surprised by the question. "Yeah. How did you know that?"

"She told me earlier to meet her there," Case replies. "She might have something for me."

TWELVE TWENTY

THE HOUSE WAS A FRIGHTENING SIGHT in the early morning. It looked worse in the height of day. And now, in the middle of the night, it's abysmal, bleak and skull-like.

Case goes around back. Much is the same as it was before. There's the picnic table put into order after what happened with the hawks, and there's Abby's lawn chair sitting under the tree. The doors are shut, and the curtains, though torn in places, are pulled closed as much as they can be.

Case creeps closer to peer through the gaps. There's a lamp on in the den, illuminating Steph. She's on the couch, half wrapped in a thin blanket, reading like she said she'd be.

Just as Case is about to knock on the window, she hears a noise from across the yard. When she turns toward the trees, she sees another flashlight beam. She assumes it's Abby, hiding near the tree line, trying to get her attention. Case jogs in that direction and then collides with something—some*one*, much bigger than wispy Abby. She still has her pocketknife, and she swipes it sideways, awkwardly. Somehow, she manages to halt the arc of her arm midway when she sees, directly in her line of sight, the word TIMMY's embroidered in yellow on a red button-up shirt.

"Jesus!" gasps Case, gaining her footing and pulling Bryan deeper into the trees. "What are you doing out here?"

"I changed the tire," Bryan says. "I tried to pull closer, but there's a stalled car in the driveway."

"Yeah, I know."

"I walked up the lane," Bryan goes on to say, "but didn't want to get too close to the house, so I stuck to the sides. Where does this path go? To the Brazos?"

"Eventually, but—"

Case doesn't get to finish her thought. Bryan's attention has snapped away, and he's thrown his hand up between them, urging Case to be quiet. His chin tilts slightly as he listens for something.

Case does the same. She listens for footfalls or familiar whispers or Abby's little breathy coughs or gum smacks. As she regrips her knife in her sweaty palm, she almost expects a hawk to come bursting out of the trees straight toward them. At this point, nothing would surprise her.

Case starts to edge toward the side of the path, but Bryan grabs her by the upper arm and pulls her back. It's her arm with the scars, which Case hates people touching, but before she can yank it away, Bryan leans in.

"Hogs," he rasps.

Case melts. It really does feel like her skin is sliding off, like the soles of her shoes are liquefying, oozing into the ground. She listens more closely and hears exactly what she doesn't want to hear: the rooting, the scraping, the grunts.

"It'll pass us," Bryan says.

He sounds sure, but how could he know? The hog shuffling around in the underbrush knows Bryan and Case are there. Animals know these things, especially ones as scent-centered as wild hogs. It'll only pass them if it doesn't consider them a threat, but usually anything—big or small—that creeps around in the dark is considered a threat.

Case desperately wants to be in Bryan's truck again. She wants a do-over. She lets herself imagine for a second that they're on the interstate, headed to her aunt's apartment in Fort Worth, and that she's so fast asleep she's snoring grossly in the passenger seat.

Instead, the hog is getting closer, weaving through the trees, stomping across the fallen limbs, and raking through the dirt. It's somewhere back behind them, between the house and where they're standing.

All this time, Case has been facing Bryan, staring at the threads in his embroidery, and it's only now that she looks away. She does see . . . *something*, something shadowed and moving slow. It's not nearly as big as the hog she came across that summer evening a few years ago, the one that chased her down and caused her to collide with Andrea, but maybe memory and time have made that first hog bigger, badder, more ugly. This one, though, seems less intimidating. The noises it produces are still ugly, but somehow the way it moves is less threatening. It's not turning its big, monstrous head in their direction. Case can't see the gleam of a tusk peeking up and out from its lower lip.

She's thinking that Bryan was right, that it *will* pass them by, that everything will be fine. But then out from the trees steps a larger, more brutal version of the same animal. That second animal turns on Bryan and Case, and Case knows, immediately: it's a mother, protecting her child, and they are *fucked*.

Bryan knows it too, understands the massive pile of shit they've gotten themselves into, and he pushes Case down the path.

"Run!" he cries. "Go, *go*."

Case runs, and Bryan follows. Within moments, they pass the chicken house, which is silent and closed up for the night. Beyond that is the crooked cedar that leads to the other path, and Case pulls Bryan toward it. Branches sting her face. Even though she's tripping on whatever thick and twisted things carpet the forest floor, she makes it to the rougher, narrower path.

The river is close. Through one last line of trees ahead. Case pushes through but then goes into a slide. Her boots have hit mud. The soles can't find traction. Bryan barrels into Case from behind, but instead of causing her to fall, he catches her around the waist and manages to haul her upright.

Together, tangled in a weird embrace, they spin. They scan the trees. Case clamps her hand over her mouth to hush her loud and panicked breaths. She needs to use her ears, but they're taking a while to tune in. Where is the hog? Where is it? All she can hear is the sound of the river. It's moving fast, but it's not loud here, like it was at the trestle bridge. It sounds like a kitchen faucet not turned off all the way, or the hush-hum that comes from a white-noise machine.

The mother hog hasn't followed them this far. If it had, they would hear it. There's something else nearby, though. Case and Bryan turn in unison again, this time away from the trees. Voices are coming from the direction of the river—not from all the way across the water, but from just down the bank, around and out of sight.

"I told you. She's not here."

"For real. She's long gone by now."

It was Kendall who spoke first, followed by Abby. Case thinks that Abby's maybe talking louder than she needs to, like she's hoping Case is lurking around and hearing every word being spoken. This, again, is Abby being helpful-not-helpful.

"I just want to be sure."

That last voice was Troy's.

"Whatever, but I'm not crossing that water," Abby says.

"It might not be that deep," Troy says.

"I'm not crossing that water, Troy. *You* do it. Or Kendall can do it."

Kendall doesn't reply.

"Abby," Troy begins, "since *you* let her out, you can't complain about this."

"I didn't let her out," Abby protests, her voice booming. "Why are you two blaming me for everything? All this shit started when you both lured Charlie down to the river."

"Lure," Kendall says. "*Please*."

"You knew what you were doing," Abby counters, "and you knew Andrea would be the only one of us to try and go in to help him."

Case is still pressed against Bryan's chest, but now she feels his entire body go tense. He shifts slightly to search Case's eyes.

Flashlight beams approach. Bryan notices them and gently tries to pull Case away, deeper into the trees, but then they're both startled by a buzzing sound at Case's hip. Case looks down and sees her pocket glowing. Somehow, she's found a sliver of cell connectivity, and her phone has decided to start working. It's great, but it's terrible. The ringer is off, but the sound is still loud, discordant with the other night noises.

There's another buzz, and Case fumbles. She steps away from Bryan, then switches the knife she's holding to her other hand, so she can yank out her phone, see that the time is 12:20, and read the two messages that just came in, one right after the other—from, of all people, her mother.

Honey, just got your message.

Followed by, *Everything ok?*

Leave it to Case's mother to send her short words of concern at the worst possible time.

"*So* not okay, Mom," Case whispers.

Bryan clears his throat. He bumps his shoulder lightly against hers.

When Case looks up from her glowing screen, she sees Kendall, Abby, and Troy facing her, standing a few feet away. Abby is scrunching up her face like she's so very disappointed in Case.

"Who are *you*?" Kendall asks, pointing her flashlight beam at the center of Bryan's chest.

When Abby finally shifts her focus from Case to Bryan, her head tilts slightly to the side. If she's the only one of the housemates who ever goes to the store, goes to get gas and pick up ice, she must recognize him, the boy behind the counter at Timmy's.

Again, Bryan nudges Case, then motions with his chin toward Troy, who is holding a shotgun by his side.

Case could say *Abby told me everything*, but she doesn't. Instead, she pretends like the conversation in the car never happened.

"What happened?" Case demands. "We heard you talking. Charlie went into the water. Drea went after him."

"That's what happened," Troy replies. His voice seems slower than normal, sludgy. "Charlie went into the water. Andrea went after him."

"And that's it?" Case asks. "You just let that happen?"

"We looked for them," Troy insists. "We ran down the riverbank, tried to get into the water, but it was too high."

Case remembers what Troy told her earlier, that he'd die by drowning. At the time, Case thought he was talking shit, just trying to agitate her, but now she wonders if Troy believes it and lives in fear of water. Right now, he sure looks like he's being plagued by a bad omen.

Case shines her light near Troy's face. His pupils are shrunken into pinpricks, and his eyes are red. His sleeves are rolled up, revealing dried mud spackled across both his forearms. He's wearing rubber boots, also splashed with mud.

He looks like he's emerged from the river, crawled out of the muck. A lot like Case. Not so pristine anymore.

"I came back the next morning," Troy goes on to say, "when the water levels were down. And the morning after that. I *tried*. There was *nothing*."

Troy takes another step forward—a weird, wobbly one—and then lets out a slight gurgling laugh. He's acting like he's drunk, or . . . *wait*.

This is the painkiller thief. Troy is out here in the dark, feeling vulnerable, holding a gun—and *high*.

"I don't like . . . ," Troy begins, scratching at his hair with his dirty fingers. "If only he'd never come and disrupted everything."

So much disruption. The ground exploding, mass evacuations, strangers coming to his supposed sanctuary, rivers sweeping people away, birds flying into rooms, a sympathetic traitor of a girlfriend.

"This all happened about a week ago," Bryan says. "That

was when they last opened the dam. You could've called someone, and they might've found them."

"You're a liar," Troy says, ignoring Bryan and pointing his flashlight at Case. "You lied when you said the troopers were coming. They'd be here by now."

"Either that or Abby lied," Kendall offers. "That seems to be all she's done all day."

Abby snickers.

"Forget Charlie," Kendall goes on to say. "*Andrea* should never have been here. She shouldn't have been invited into the car that day, and now it doesn't even really matter that she's gone, because she didn't *do* anything. She wasn't necessary."

"Necessary?" Case echoes.

"Ugh, Kendall," Abby scoffs. "You are *such* an asshole."

"Yes, *necessary*," Kendall replies. "Troy is *necessary* because this is his property. Abby has the car."

"Had," Abby interjects. "*Had* the car."

Kendall goes on: "I keep the house in order. Steph helps me and tends to the chickens. Andrea just went into the woods every day and came back out with a bunch of shitty stories."

Next to Case, Bryan makes a choking sound.

"Oh, come on, Kendall!" shouts Abby. "We're all *fucking* unnecessary. We live in the middle of fucking nowhere, talk to no one and contribute to *nothing*."

"What are we supposed to contribute to, Abby?" Kendall demands. "Huh? The world out there is *fucked*."

"We can't stay here forever, Kendall!" Abby says. "And you can't just plan on attacking everyone who shows up."

Abby and Kendall continue sniping at each other, and Case slumps against Bryan. Her headache is roaring back. She squeezes her eyes shut for a moment.

When she reopens them, she sees something she hadn't seen before, or maybe something that just materialized from the water. It's on the ground, right behind Troy, at the edge of the river. It looks like a tree branch, or a piece of a tree branch swept up by the water and then caught up in the muck by the bank. It bobs and shimmies a bit as the current tries to pull it away, but then it does something a tree branch doesn't do: it fights against the current, lifts its little head, looks around, and starts to wind the entire length of its body up and out of the water.

Case freezes. She can feel Bryan looking at her, trying to figure out what's going wrong, what's happening. Case scans the rest of the muddy ground by the river's edge. There are more. There have to be. Water moccasins aren't solitary. They swarm. They make nests.

"What?" Bryan whispers.

"Snake," Case says.

It's moving more quickly now, more deliberately snake-like, slinking its way through the mud toward an unsuspecting Troy, until it's close enough to nuzzle its head against the rubber of his boot. As quietly as he can, Bryan reaches into his pocket, pulls out his keys, and hands them to Case. Why Bryan does this, Case has no idea, but she takes them anyway, then slides them into her pocket along with the rest of the things she's collected over the course of the day.

"What?" Abby asks, catching on that something isn't right. She swings her flashlight in a wide, wild arc. "What is it?"

"Hey," Bryan says to Troy, gesturing to the ground. "I don't want to freak you out, but . . ."

Troy is slow on the uptake. He blinks lazily, makes a confused face, and then, finally, looks to his feet. It takes a moment for him to register the snake, but when he does he jumps and lets out a loud cry.

While Troy is distracted, Bryan lunges forward and tries to grab the shotgun. Both boys have their hands around it. The barrel is pointed down when the first shot goes off. There's an explosion of mud.

"Go!" Bryan shouts to Case. "Take the truck. Get out of here."

At first, Case can't move. She watches Troy elbow Bryan in the gut and Bryan fall back. She sees Kendall rip the gun away from Troy and turn toward him and Bryan. Then Kendall spins toward Case and tries to get her footing on the slick earth.

"Case, go!" Bryan coughs out.

But Case can't go. All the running she's done in her life, and Case has suddenly lost her legs. They're stuck—stuck in this ground, stuck in the mud.

It's Abby who comes to the rescue. She rushes up and shoves Kendall sideways. A shot goes off with a boom, wide to left, and the bright flash from the barrel of the gun is what shakes Case from her stupor. She finds her feet and runs, just as Kendall digs into her pockets for more shells.

As Case bursts through the trees in the direction of the path, she hears another shout—from a boy—then a splash. That's the moment when Case feels something pummel into her, nearly knocking her down—she knows from the blond hair whipping past that it's Steph.

Case continues on. Within seconds, she's at the crooked cedar. She ducks, then pivots around the tree. Her feet find the wider, smoother path. It isn't muddy here, but she's slow; the soles of her boots are still slick from the river mud. She knows the chicken house is ahead, but she stops, gasping for air. She can't do this. She can't leave Bryan. She can't lose another friend, even one gained so recently, to the water.

Case spins around, but there, in the path, is Kendall.

"What happened back there?" Case asks. "At the water? Who fell in?"

Kendall doesn't reply, just lifts the shotgun and aims it, again, at Case.

There's a sound from the trees, loud and monstrous enough to catch Kendall's attention.

The two hogs emerge, the mother and child. The mother charges. Kendall doesn't have time to scream before she falls.

Almost immediately, there's a shotgun blast, a ball of bright white followed by the stink of gunpowder. Case jolts as a heavy and coarse *thing* barrels past her leg. As she tilts sideways, she sees Abby and Steph coming up the path.

"Go, go!" Case calls out to Abby. "Get to the house. Steph, *go!*"

Abby follows the command. She vanishes quickly down the dark path, and Case spins around—in one complete clockwise circle, then in another. She's searching the ground, looking for the brightness of denim against dirt, or blond hair in a braid.

What she sees first is Kendall's palm-up hand, the one that's been covered all day in crusted flour and coyote fur.

After the hand comes the arm, then the shoulder, then the head, neck, chest. Everything is there. Everything is fine. Because the light of the moon makes the whole scene look eerie, Case can't tell if Kendall has paled, but her eyes look normal, and she's not sucking in strange, uneven breaths.

Then Case sees the blood. She sees it on Steph's hands first—Steph, who didn't run to the house with Abby, but who is kneeling next to her sister.

"What happened?" Case lunges toward the girl. She lands hard on her knees on the rocky earth. "Where?"

Steph shakes her head. The blood isn't hers. Again, Case scans Kendall's body. Before, her eyes stopped at Kendall's chest, at the sight of it rising and falling, but now it goes lower. There's her stomach, and then: so much blood. It's coating the top part of Kendall's leg. It's actually seeping out, gently bubbling, like a black fountain.

Case gags not at the sight, but at the *smell*: fresh like new rain, but also tinged with decay.

Stretched out on its side next to Kendall is one of the hogs, dead. It's the young one. Its darkness blends in with the dark ground. Case can't imagine an animal that small doing that amount of damage to Kendall's leg. The mother must've gored her, then somehow, Kendall got off a shot that struck the smaller hog.

Case still has the rope strung on her belt loop. She unravels it and does her best to wind it around Kendall's upper thigh. With all the blood coating her fingers, she doesn't think she's able to tie it very tight.

"What's happening?" Steph asks.

Case looks to the girl. She doesn't know the right thing to say. With a wound like this, even with the help of a makeshift tourniquet, Kendall will probably bleed out within minutes. "I . . ."

"I wish you would leave," the girl mumbles.

"You need to go back to the house," Case says, her voice breaking. "There's another hog."

The mother was angry to begin with but is now probably whipped up into a fury.

"You go," Steph says, defiantly. "I'm not leaving."

Case stands on wobbly legs. "There's another hog," she repeats.

"No," Steph replies. "There's not."

The girl says it with such certainty that, for a split second, Case questions herself. She saw two animals—or at least she knows she *heard* two—their grunts layered on top of one another. She felt one rush past her. Didn't she?

She did. Yes. She's sure she did. Case looks at her own legs, pats around. Mercifully, she's somehow intact.

Case searches the ground for the shotgun and finds it a couple of feet from Kendall's head, as if the force of the blast had thrown it up and out of her hands. She doesn't risk another glance at Kendall's eyes—or at her chest—as she fumbles through the dying girl's front pockets, which themselves are soaking through with blood. Finding what she was hoping to find—a small cache of shotgun shells—she stands. The chambers of the gun, as she thought, are empty. Case rattles in a couple of shells and then snaps the barrel into place.

"I'm going to get help," she says to Steph. Case pulls out her phone and drops it onto the ground next to Steph. "Use this. Try to find reception." Then again, Case says, "You should go back to the house."

Steph says nothing, just looks to her sister. She puts a bloody hand flat between Kendall's collarbones.

"Steph," Case starts, "I think—" She's cut off by a scream.

It's Abby. Case spins in the direction of the sound.

There's another scream, and Case is on the move, running as fast as she can, down a path she can barely see. Occasionally, she veers too far to the side, causing the slick soles of her boots to land awkwardly against rocks or tree roots.

"Abby!" cries Case. "Abby, *where?*"

Case is headed toward the chicken house, but when the slumped red shack comes into view, she stops. There's no Abby and no hog. Just when Case is about to take off in the direction of the main house, she hears Abby shout her name. It comes from the trees, from the path that leads to the burn pile.

How Abby ended up there, of all places, Case has no idea. It doesn't really matter. Case heads that way, but she has to slow her pace, because she can barely see the narrow strip of trod grass under her feet. Then, appearing sooner than she remembers from before, she's faced with the tall stalks of Johnsongrass, which wave in the gentlest of night breezes.

"Abby!" shouts Case.

The response is a wet, angry snarl—not human, but hog.

Case falters. Her legs go weak again, but she steadies herself by gripping the shotgun to her chest with both hands. She listens for Abby. The girl is making a screechy whine, like a drawn-out flat note. Case pushes through the thick grass.

Abby is standing on the far side of the ash pile. The first thing Case notices are Abby's bare legs. Their color is strange in the moonlight—a streaky, swirly painted gray. The clouds in the distance flash with lightning.

"Where?" Case asks.

Abby barely moves. The fingers on her right hand sort of twitch to the side. She looks so small, so thin, made of air. If the wind blows, Abby will turn to dust, and that dust will rise, then swirl, then return to the circle of ash.

Case marches forward, stepping through the burn pile. When she gets to the other side, she shifts the gun to her right hand, and then loops her and Abby's elbows together.

"Okay," she says, tugging Abby closer. Then after a moment: "We need to move, get back to the house."

Abby nods, and together the girls take one step toward the path. And another. Case reaches out her hand, the one that's still holding the gun. Her bloody fingers graze the stalks of grass, ready to push them aside, when something tears out of its hiding place from behind, near the place where Abby was standing only seconds ago. The girls turn together. Their elbows come unlocked. Like before, like with Kendall, Case sees a dark blur whipping past.

Abby cries out, starts to sink, and Case fumbles to grab her and hold her upright. The hog has passed, disappeared again into the grass, but it might circle back. Case drags Abby along.

"What happened?" Case asks.

"My leg." Abby sinks farther, fast losing the ability to stand, even with Case's help.

Case braces herself, and glances down. The wound, thank god, isn't like Kendall's. It's not at the thigh but in the meat of Abby's calf. If it was deep, Case might even be able to see a shine of bone, but all she sees is red muscle and black blood.

They have to get out of here. Case can use the sleeve of her shirt as a tourniquet, since there's no more rope. She can sling Abby's arm over her shoulder and carry her out, even though it'll be slow going. But then there's the hog—still out there, hunting them.

Case wipes her bloody hands on her jeans and looks up. There's something happening with the sky. The approaching storm is playing tricks with the light. Blowing it up, it seems. There are moments when everything is spotlit, followed by moments when everything is dark.

It's in one of those spotlit moments that she can see the hog—standing at the edge of the other side of the small, charred clearing. It's watching her, patiently, like it's waiting to be acknowledged. Like Abby, the hog is also streaked with ash, and when it snorts, white dust puffs from its nostrils. Case raises the barrel of the gun to the sky and shoots, hoping the boom will startle the hog away.

It has the opposite effect. The hog charges forward, and Case has to aim quickly and pray the bullet flies true. As she fires, the butt of the rifle smashes into her shoulder so hard she loses her balance and stumbles to the side.

There's a spray of blood, but the hog doesn't drop—not right away. It lopes forward a few feet, then falls on its front legs. It tries to stand, then falls again, then rubs its face in the ash angrily, like it's trying to scrape out the shot from its head. Case looks away. The hog is dying, but she can't just stand there and watch it. She drops the gun and tries to tear off the sleeve of her shirt, which doesn't really work. She then takes off her boots and strips off both her socks.

Knotting them together, she crouches in front of Abby and works to tie the fabric above the girl's knee.

"Can you walk?" Case asks, shoving her feet into her boots. "Can you please try?"

It's the worst question. Abby can barely stand.

Still, the girl places her toe on the ground. But when she tries to bear weight, she sobs and collapses. She sits, then leans onto her elbows, then finally lies down, draping her arm across her face as if to shade her eyes from the oddly flashing sky.

"I hate it here," Abby mumbles. "What am I supposed to do?"

"Wait," Case demands. "Just wait."

Case grabs the gun from where she dropped it, reloads it with more of the shells she took from Kendall, and shoves it into Abby's hands.

"You can't leave!" One of Abby's hands releases the gun and whips out to grip Case at the elbow.

"I'll be back," Case insists. "If you see anything, just aim and shoot."

Abby tries to huff out a breath, but it comes out shaky with pain. Case doesn't think she'll ever forgive Abby for everything she's done and not done, but she does think that Abby should be saved—that everyone deserves to be dragged out of a shitty situation.

"I swear I'll come back," Case says. "Thank you for Drea's letter—for giving it to me."

Abby doesn't reply, but her grip loosens enough for Case to pull away. Again, Case runs.

She passes Abby's car, then Bryan's truck, and then skids to a stop when she sees headlights approaching from the end of the lane. It's an SUV, with SHERIFF'S DEPT painted on the front end of the hood, right above the grille. There's a loud beep that causes Case to jolt, and then, almost immediately, the lights mounted to the top of the SUV start flashing.

Case can see the deputy inside, shouting something into the radio before opening her door and taking a step forward. One of her hands is extended toward Case, while the other is braced against the holster on her hip. Case puts her hands up, and the deputy's eyes go wide at the sight of the blood smeared all over Case's arms.

"Hogs," Case rasps. She's too quiet. The deputy is still too far away. She doesn't hear her.

"Andrea?" the deputy calls.

Case feels dizzy.

"Are you Andrea Soto?" the deputy asks, approaching.

Case tries to respond, but nothing comes out.

"Andrea." The deputy is trying to be kind, to keep her tone calm and reassuring. "Andrea, it's okay. You're all right now. I'm glad we found you. Your mom wants you to know that she misses you."

The deputy smiles. Case smiles back.

PART THREE:
DAY

EIGHT

WHEN THE CAR PULLS UP, Case is leaning against the back bumper of a state trooper's cruiser, reading another text from Bryan.

Been here for hours, he says. *Will keep you posted.*

The driver stops the car and frowns. He's confused, understandably. Case puts her phone in her pocket and gives him a half-hearted wave, which she doubts is reassuring. She's filthy, exhausted to the point of delirious, and has an itchy blanket wrapped around her shoulders.

The sun has been up for over an hour, but that doesn't mean it's bright. The whole sky is acorn brown and covered by a thin scrim of clouds. It doesn't smell like ash, though, or burning trash. It smells like grass and earth, the nothing scent of how a summer morning in the country should smell.

Case is ready to go. She shakes off the blanket, places it on top of the trooper's trunk, grabs her duffel bag from down by her feet, and heads to the car.

"Is everything . . . all right?" the driver asks as Case sinks into the back seat. "Are you sure you're supposed to be leaving?"

It's a fair question. There are four police vehicles parked in the lane. They belong to officers from the local sheriff's department and also troopers from the state. There were even more cars than this earlier, plus ambulances and a fire truck. Case's head was swirling from all the flashing lights—red and blue and white—and from the blips and static of the radios.

"It's fine," Case replies. "We can go."

She's been here for hours, as rescue workers plucked the roommates from the woods, one at a time. Case directed them to where everyone was. The first one out was Abby. She was in the most serious condition, bleeding and in shock.

Troy was next, which was a surprise. Case didn't think she'd ever see him again, that the river might've swallowed him up and that his body might've been swept all the way into a different county by now. During Troy's scuffle with Bryan, the water moccasin *did* bite him, and he *did* fall into the water. Bryan, of course, because he is kind and brave and a lot like Drea, went in after him and managed to drag him back to shore.

By the time the medics hauled Troy to where the ambulances were parked, his leg was already wrapped. Case didn't want to be one of those curious creeps, but she did wish she could see the skin on Troy's leg, and if his veins were streaked with poison. Maybe there were bite marks— two perfect holes.

Steph came out with the body of her sister, looking like an awful little wraith in her bloody, mud-strewn clothes.

There were a couple of twigs stuck in her hair, with some leaves still attached. Almost like a crown, Case thought.

Case wondered what would happen to Steph when this was over, imagined her returning to this house in a few days, maybe a week—tending to the chickens, maybe planting a garden. She had to have watched her sister enough to know how to coax sourdough starter into dough, then bake that into bread.

As Steph passed by on her way to being checked out by the medics, Case asked her if she'd found any more of Drea's writing.

The look Steph gave Case was withering.

"It's important," Case insisted, undeterred. "Or you could just tell me where to maybe look."

Steph still didn't say anything, and Case was reminded of what she'd told Bryan back in the truck—something about how the roommates might be terrible, but she wasn't all that stellar herself.

Bryan stuck around for a while. His cough had come back, more violently than before, and the paramedics had to hook him up to oxygen for a while before he could give his statement. After that, he took his keys from Case and left in his truck to meet with different investigators at the sheriff's department.

Case spent most of the rest of the night sitting at the old table in the kitchen. She talked and waited and talked. At one point, she heard dogs barking, and she knew the police had started searching the property.

Eventually, Case got light-headed. She reached into her duffel bag, which she'd retrieved earlier from Bryan's truck, pulled out her empty prescription bottle, and handed it to the detective who was interviewing her. He'd looked confused, but then Case rolled up the sleeve of her shirt, exposing her scars. The man jumped up, went out to the medics, and returned with a couple of pills.

"They're not the same," he said. "But they should work."

Case took them gratefully, and chased them with a glassful of water.

The investigator finally asked if she needed a ride somewhere. Case said no, that she already had one. The investigator told Case to keep her phone close, that they'd be in touch.

"What will happen to the house?" Case asked.

"I'm not sure," the investigator replied. "It'll probably stay a crime scene for a while. But after that, I don't know."

As Case's car turns off the lane and onto the county road, she's still thinking about the house and what might become of it. She can't take it away from Troy's family, or pluck the tiles from the bathroom wall one by one, or tear up the floorboards, or rip the ivy from the exterior, but she wishes she could. She thinks, though, that the house is cursed now. The land and animals won't leave it alone. The air around it will be unbreathable. The nearby river will continue to rise. Vicious birds will swoop in from the skies, and the snakes will slither from the murky water. The ghost of a girl will be there too, making sure everyone gets what they deserve.

As the car pulls out onto the road, Bryan sends another text: *You'll be happy to know that, as expected, I did not get fired! Come visit next time you're in town.*

Case grins and then rolls down her window. In the distance, she can hear the search dogs barking, all together, as one. They've found something.

ACKNOWLEDGMENTS

I am grateful for my teachers, students, friends, family, readers, colleagues, and champions. None of my books would exist without the encouragement and guidance of my editor, Krestyna Lypen. This novel felt particularly nebulous in its early stages, and I appreciate Krestyna's ability to have seen through the muck. Of course, so many thanks to everyone who has worked on my books at Algonquin Young Readers and Workman, past and present.

Claire Anderson-Wheeler is my brilliant agent, and I would be lost without her keen eye and support.

The English department at Southern Methodist University gifted me the opportunity to travel out of state, hunker down in the mountains, and do crucial work on revisions of this novel at their campus in Taos, New Mexico. This time and space was invaluable.

Kara Thomas, Rory Power, and Nova Ren Suma all read early versions of this novel and generously offered their praise.

Thank you to my husband, Jeff Schulze, for his unwavering support and for his refusal to let me write bad sentences. Always and forever, I am grateful for and inspired by my young son and bright star, Guy.

The inspiration for this novel came from a variety of sources and places, in particular the 1955 film *Bad Day at Black Rock* (in which the protagonist, played by Spencer Tracy, arrives at a small town full of hostile inhabitants looking for an old friend), as well as the novels *The Likeness* by Tana French (featuring an old house in the woods filled with cagey people) and *Lonesome Dove* by Larry McMurtry (featuring, among so many other amazing things, a river full of snakes). Certainly, I was also inspired by Palo Pinto County, Texas, and the Brazos River.

The volcanic activity and its immediate aftermath described in this novel were inspired by the 1815 eruption of Mount Tambora, in what is now Indonesia. The results of the eruption were cataclysmic, causing global environmental disasters such as drought, crop failure, and drastic changes in weather patterns, including, yes, pink snowfall in the summer. This massive event was also said to have shaken some people's notions of faith and spiritual balance and is known to have inspired the work of writers such as Lord Byron and Mary Shelley.